Charm Town

First Novel in the Charm Town Series

HUNTER WILLIAM

CHARM TOWN. Copyright © 2016 by Hunter William

M & M Publishing
6710 Laurel Bowie Road
Suite 2114
Bowie, Maryland 20716

Library of Congress Control Number: 2016913587

ISBN 978-0-9979500-0-7

Cover Design by Heavy Hitter Designs, LLC.

Interior Design and Editing by TWASolutions.com

Printed in the United States of America

First Edition

DEDICATION

To all gifted and talented young people in urban communities who never realized their potential and life's possibilities.

To all grieving parents who have lost a child to violence, illness or otherwise.

To all dedicated youth professionals who care about children and labor every day to shine a bright light in a dark place.

Acknowledgements

Francis and Betty—Thank you for a lifetime of lessons, support and faith.

Mark—Thank you for being the best example of commitment, patience, and sacrifice I have known. A quiet strength, I admire you from afar every day.

Michael—Thank you for your love and your courage to be your own person and do things your own way. It's heartening to watch your growth.

Bill—Thank you for your support, encouragement, love and dedication to your family. Your perseverance is an example for all. The biggest thank you is for our children.

Mayson and Maxwell—Thank you for being the greatest "little people" in the world. I hope this project makes you a third proud of your mommy as I am of you each day. Always pursue your dreams and passions for they are possible and know there simply will never be enough space on this earth to contain the love I have for you.

Family and Friends—Thank you for your inspiration, motivation, support, criticism, prayers, questions, and answers. You uplift me in ways you cannot imagine and I am grateful.

New Friends & Readers—Thank you for being here, in this space, reading my story.

BOOK 1

THE START OF THE SCHOOL YEAR TO THE CHRISTMAS VACATION

Chapter One

Her name was Peyton Stanfield. Professionally confident and intimately vulnerable, she was a social worker in the Charm Town "tough as nails" School District. Thirty-five years into life, sophisticated, beautiful, loyal, committed, fun loving, and dedicated to her work, many considered her a skilled, knowledgeable, "knows her shit" clinician who, as some told it, attended all the right schools: Howard University, Northwestern University, and Smith College. A Phi Beta Kappa, none of her classmates in social work school presented a diagnostic impression or designed a genogram more detailed than she could. Always cheerful and sweet, classmates and friends considered her a smart girl; never one to make bad choices or go against the grain of whatever society stamped as right or wrong. She knew to avoid wrong choices or attracting the unsavory characters of the world. They never imagined her feeling emotionally fragile, occasionally manic, and sometimes willing to do almost anything for the attention, approval, and desire of men. Her secret was while school and studying was easy for her, love relationships were awkward, difficult, and sometimes hurtful.

The youngest and only daughter in a family of six, she grew up on the Western Shore, in a small town where everyone knew everyone. She had three older brothers who were always her protectors. That was the way of the Stanfield boys. They had a reputation of athletically gifted and defenders of themselves and those close to them. Once, when Peyton was harassed in high school by two female upperclassmen over a boy who attended another high school who expressed an interest in dating her, it was her brothers who immediately sprung to her defense, confronted the girls and threatened to beat them up if they laid a hand on their sister. Football was their sport of choice, and their physiques illustrated their extensive time in the weight room. People called them the "new version of the Incredible Hulk" and knew not to start any smack because it never ended well for them.

Town people viewed the Stanfields as the prominent Black family. They had money, were highly educated, and hosted some of the best social parties. One would get good potato salad, fresh grilled fish, and moist cornbread at the Stanfield house. Her parents graduated from the prestigious Freeman's State College, the sole historically Black college in the state, long known for its ability to educate young, gifted, Black minds. Her mother, Jacqueline, the family's saving grace, was a teacher who spent her entire career instructing other people's children, wanting them to do well, and make something of themselves. She encouraged her students to leave their comfort zone, attend college and meet, as she called it, "new blood." Having grown up in a large, urban city, her family was shocked when she moved to the country after college graduation, rejected promising job opportunities, converted to Methodist, and married Thomas Stanfield who settled in a farm town. Her mother was the one who was present through the hardships of being the only Black, little girl in her class teased, ignored, or not invited to birthday parties. She and her mother enjoyed what Peyton considered a good surface relationship. As long as they didn't speak about the serious topics of life, their relationship was golden. The subjects of love and lust weren't easy or comfortable topics for Jacqueline. Retired from teaching, she and Peyton spoke often, as she called most nights and sometimes during the day.

Peyton's father, Thomas, a bank executive, was rarely home and often traveled with a suitcase or two that remained semi-packed in the house. Years later, she realized her father, most likely, enjoyed multiple affairs with women but she never heard her mother speak about it. She did remember one bad argument where they screamed at each other behind their closed bedroom door, but Peyton didn't understand everything they said, although she heard "that woman" and "all I gave up to be here with you." Her mother was angry afterward and her parents ignored each other and did not speak for days.

When her father was home, he wasn't attentive to his daughter or inquired about her young life. He spent much of his scarce time running around to ball games with her brothers. Her vivid memories of him were limited to Easter and Christmas, and her life transitions of high school and college graduations. Birthdays came and went, sometimes without an acknowledgment from him, except for the generic card from Peoples Drug store her mother gave with both their names signed by her. Peyton and her father continued to have the same relationship in her adult years as her childhood. They rarely spoke, usually when she visited because he almost never visited her, and neither seemed to find the time to telephone, except on rare occasions. Their relationship was bothersome to her and she thought of confronting him and blaming him for her life's missteps, but realized there was no point to such tirades. She knew nothing would change, and accepting her father for the man he was, proved easier. Leaving her cash, stocks, and bonds in his will was the only remarkable memory of their relationship. She was shocked when she received the phone call from his attorney, informing her of the will's existence and its terms. He died when Peyton was in graduate school of heart disease. Her mother chose to remain living alone in the house they built before Peyton was born.

Her childhood was carefree, full of school activities, friends, sports, and fun times with her relatives. Her family's social position oftentimes allotted Peyton a *pass*, never looked upon by her friends and teachers as anything other than well bred and prepared for the world. She and her brothers were members of the prestigious Jack and Jill of America and she was crowned Miss Alpha at age sixteen.

In high school, she was a social person with many friends, although dating was uneasy for her. She didn't have a frame of reference, except for what she saw on television soap operas and she loved soap operas. The love stories of Victor and Nikki of *The Young and the Restless* and Luke and Laura of *General Hospital* were seductive. On those shows, love and happiness were certain and always seemed to work for everyone. Awkward in appearance and dress, boys didn't flock to her as they did other girls in her school. She was aware some girls had "reputations," but didn't fully understand the meaning. Feeling uncomfortable and sometimes unattractive, she shied away from the popular kids and always found her way to the back of the room of parties and hated walking in front of the crowd at her school's sporting activities. She and her parents never discussed boys, kisses, or sex. A super conservative, religious couple, she could not recall one time in her childhood when she witnessed her parents in an affectionate, intimate moment. She had no idea of how to respond to a boy when approached, except for what she learned from her good friend, Tamara. Having met during a joint community service project for their schools, they quickly bonded over preparing and serving meals to homeless families.

Tamara was loads of fun, always ready for a good time and the girl most talked about years later at the class reunion. She had friends from each of the six high schools in the district. Her weekends consisted of invitations to this party or that gathering and she enjoyed the freedom to attend whichever event she preferred. The belle of the party, she garnered a harmless reputation of bringing the fun wherever she went. Her parents, like Peyton's, didn't pay much attention to her life. She didn't seem to have any inhibitions or fears, and Peyton secretly wanted to be like her. With Tamara's personality and experiences, she never had a problem attracting and keeping boys. Her parents were divorced and didn't get along, so she took advantage of her dad's desire of always wanting to embarrass her mother when it came to gifts and money for her. Peyton knew Tamara hated that her parents despised each other because she would cry and say she didn't want her parents to be mad at her when she took the other's side during arguments or wanted to spend time with the other. It was easier for her to busy herself with a social life than to get her parents to interact and talk with each other. Peyton liked her parents, but always wondered how two people, who obviously *once upon a time* had affection, ended up on the road of despise and didn't seem to care about the impact upon their daughter. She loved spending time over Tamara's house, where no rules existed, except for the time her boyfriend, Byron, came over with one of his friends, looking to score. They were alone and Peyton was nervous when Byron's friend, Larry, kept rubbing on her legs and asking her to go upstairs to the bedroom. After thirty minutes of constantly pushing him away and pretending to look at something on television, he got the message and left to retrieve Byron to leave. She supposed he figured if he wasn't being laid, neither would Byron. Tamara seemed upset, but Peyton was relieved and grateful when they left. The two friends shared many laughs, cries over boys, Friday night parties, their first sips of alcohol and sleepovers in high school. After graduation, they attended different colleges, drifted apart with new friends and experiences, and contact among them was lost.

Peyton's first sexual experience, influenced by bathroom girlfriends at school, was with a boy in the basement of his parents' house. She was seventeen and he was sixteen years old. She met him when he attended her school's homecoming football game with his stepbrother. It wasn't supposed to be sexual, but they partied one day, drank Pink Champale wine coolers, and one moment led to another. They kissed and, the next thing she knew, he pulled her shirt off and pants down, first around her ankles and then completely off. She wanted to stop him, but didn't, not wanting to disappoint him, thinking he wouldn't talk with her again and would call her a tease——a girl who pretended to want sex, but backed out when the boy was ready. That was her problem with boys: fearful she had to do what the boy wanted to do to win his approval; thus, she would feel like a part of the in crowd. Utilizing a condom, he inserted his penis into her vagina and proceeded to move in an up-and-down motion, telling her to keep her legs lifted in the air, until he stopped moving. She didn't know what happened, but he suddenly stood up, looked at her with a blank stare, and walked to the bathroom.

Peyton was horrified at the bloodstains on the towel he put down prior and embarrassed she didn't know where the blood came from or its purpose. Her mind quickly went to thoughts of the soap operas.

This isn't how Victor and Luke move when they are making love to Nikki and Laura. Why is this not fun to me? Where are the stars, soft music, and whispers in my ear? And, where is the tray with flowers and food brought to me as I lay here?

Not knowing her true feelings, he was sweet and kind to her at a time when she craved and needed male attention, desperately wanting to mirror the other girls in her class who had sex with their boyfriends. The next time she wandered into the school's bathroom to a bunch of girls bragging about having sex, she might just join in with her story. She remembered the feeling of the act, and going home that night, throwing her clothes on the floor in her bedroom and her mother coming in and talking with her as if she knew something was different about her daughter. She never asked Peyton about her actions and she never told her about them.

Her *real* high school boyfriend was Jerry, who was older, a graduate of the local community college, and worked a full-time job. She sought his approval and became sexually active with him when she visited him at his mother's house. She loved the attention he gave her and when he came to her school and picked her up in his car to go to the local Roy Rogers or Hardees restaurants. Sometimes they went to 7-Eleven for cherry Slurpees and Snickers candy bars. Some of her friends were jealous she had a boyfriend with a car. One night, he joined her and her parents for dinner at Perkins Restaurant & Bakery. It was awkward with her mother pretending to be nice and her father not saying more than three words the entire meal. They never went to dinner with her parents again. He broke up with her when she left for college and eloped with a girl she was acquainted with through other friends. She was devastated. Later, after college and graduate school, they reconnected briefly. She heard he died in a work-related accident several years ago.

Peyton's college dating experiences were memorable. She wasn't like other college girls who met the *love of her life* freshman year and refused to date other boys. Her first college boyfriend was Evan, a member of Omega Psi Phi Fraternity. He, too, was older than she was, had a car, and was an engineer assistant for Westinghouse. They connected easily, enjoyed late night dinners and action movies until he discovered Peyton was a Methodist. He asked a ton of dumb questions, made rude, ignorant comments about the denomination, and tried to persuade her to convert to Baptist. Frustrated with the tension, they broke up. Her second college sweetie was Jerome who was in the Navy and stationed at the Naval Academy. They met one night when Peyton was out clubbing with her girlfriends. He was good for her and boosted her self-confidence, always telling her she was beautiful and never pressing her for sex or any other favors college boys seemed to want. At the time, she thought she was in love with him; he was easy fun and didn't mind doing things with her and her college friends. They dated for a year until his reassignment to Spain. They remained in contact over the years when he lived in Texas with his family.

After Jerome, Peyton remained single, although she developed a hard crush on Barry who was super cute and a member of the Phi Beta Sigma fraternity. Secretly, she wanted to be with him, but never found the nerve to approach him. He was popular and she was sure he had no interest in her. All the girls liked him and she was convinced he had sex with many of them. Then there was Alphonso, who *was* having sex with many girls. Ridiculously handsome, he and Peyton developed a friendship after sharing a science class and teaming together for a group project. Surprisingly, he was extremely charming to her and never attempted to make sexual advances toward her. He walked with her after class, met her for lunch, and called at night to talk about his family's unrealistic expectations of him.

He was the dean of pledges for his fraternity and he came to her off-campus apartment late, ate her food, and fell asleep on her couch. She enjoyed the attention, but always feared if he did try something sexual with her, she would probably do or say something stupid, which would end their platonic friendship. One time, he invited her over to his apartment to watch a movie. She became uncomfortable when the Kim Basinger movie, *9½ Weeks*, started playing. She was anxious the entire time, sure that was the night he would try something. But, Alphonso sensed her uneasiness and fell asleep. They remained good friends during their college years.

These days, Peyton was single and more sexually confident, a result of self-discovery and a few good liaisons over the years. During a girls' sleepover with some of the teachers at her school, she acknowledged she had some good trysts, but considered herself a conservative girl in the bedroom. She had not met that man who could or would bring out the wild girl that existed in all girls. The past several years, she managed to attract men who weren't exciting, in or out of bed.

At this stage of her life, she hoped to meet someone special, and consider planning a family, even with someone who was not hers. She knew nowadays, independent, financially stable women were having children without being married, or in a committed situation with the father. She couldn't envision herself happily married to anyone for multiple years. She also didn't want to exert the energy needed in marriage and still wind up like many of her married girlfriends: alcoholic, depressed, overweight, and unfulfilled. That life transition wasn't for her. No longer feeling guilty about her feelings, she wanted to live her dreams and not compromise with the dreams of a husband.

A social worker in the school system was a desire of Peyton's since completing an internship in an elementary school while in graduate school at Northwestern. She enjoyed her work with children and liked the "youthful" feel of working in a school setting with other adults who cared about children. She received tremendous reward from the gratifying feeling of helping children and their families during a time of need. In her ten years with the Charm Town School District, she formed many positive relationships and was able to help a number of students overcome unimaginable obstacles. This job was unlike her childhood school experiences, and she was able to be a part of the good and bad of urban school life. In addition, it was great fun. Most of the teachers in her schools were of her peer group, which made for good times during and after school.

Life was more than comfortable for her, having no major stresses to cause her anguish. Her family was healthy and no one depended upon her for their survival. She lived in a poshly-decorated, three-bedroom townhouse, drove a luxury vehicle, traveled for fun with girlfriends and possessed the financial means to buy whatever she desired from clothes, jewelry, and bags to treating herself and friends to dinners at exclusive restaurants. She had friends in the entertainment industry who gave her VIP access to popular events. Most of her free time and weekends were spent sleeping late, eating with friends at popular brunch spots, and attending concerts, backyard barbecues, house parties and occasional school events, such as ball games and dances. Generous with her time and money to charities, she contributed annually to the Healthcare for the Homeless Fund and the Camp Achieve Summer Program Fund. She volunteered tutoring services at the YMCA, and mentored several teenage girls in her neighborhood who talked with her and wanted to know how she was able to afford nice things without a man. No longer the scared little girl from long ago, seeking attention from boys in all the wrong ways, she thought she was ready for whatever love came her way.

Chapter Two

His name was Hamilton Banks. Forty-three years old, tall, devilishly handsome, articulate, and well liked, he was a successful Jamaican entrepreneur who grew up on the streets of Charm Town beginning at age five. Before then, he lived in his home country of Jamaica with his father's parents. His mother and father, both Jamaican, were teenagers when they met by chance while on separate school trips to the Bob Marley Museum. They instantly developed an attraction and soon made excuses to be together. Within a year, Hamilton's fifteen-year-old mother, Geraldine, was pregnant by his sixteen-year-old father, Eustis. Young, naïve, and impressionable, they never married and had no knowledge of being parents to a baby. Teenage pregnancy and parenting was taboo in Jamaica, so neither Geraldine's nor Eustis's parents saw fit to talk about one of the biggest life events for both of them. Fearful of the reactions of their church priest and parish members, Geraldine's family looked upon her with disgust for having sex at an early age. Eustis's family looked upon him with disgust for getting a girl the likes of Geraldine pregnant. What would the Prime Minister's wife say? What would the members of the RJO say? She came from a poor family and his parents heavily chastised him for going against the family rule of not dating outside his social class. His family's name was tarnished, forever linked to a family of farmers and servants and not a family of government officials and sugar and rum entrepreneurs.

Geraldine's parents were from a different region of the country than Eustis's parents. An only child, she grew up in the city of Kingston with her mother who worked as a servant for the Blackwell family, owners of vacation resorts on the island. Her father died in an automobile accident when she was four years old. She was long aware of the stories depicting her father's accident as no accident, but retaliation for a fight he had with another eighteen-year-old boy over a girl who was not Geraldine's mother. From the stories she heard, Geraldine's father had a love for many girls and didn't see the need to date one girl at a time, especially if they gave attention and sexual favors.

The son of a political appointee and government official, Eustis grew up in a beautiful, affluent township outside of Kingston. When his parents learned of Geraldine's pregnancy and delivery, they insisted baby Hamilton be brought to live with them in what they considered a suitable environment away from the dangers of Kingston. Geraldine and her mother had no means in which to fight this, so baby Hamilton went to live with his father and grandparents. He enjoyed an early prosperous life filled with family trips to one of the numerous gorgeous beaches on the island and all the things children liked, such as toys, candy, games, ice cream, and books. He attended a prestigious preschool for the "favored kids" and easily made friends. He became accustomed to a life of ease and privilege.

At age five, Hamilton's paternal grandparents abruptly sent him to live with his mother who was moving to the United States. Packed up in one day, sent away, and never told why, he assumed his father and grandparents no longer wanted him, and the shame of his birth was ultimately too much for them to bear. He overheard conversations at their home about the embarrassment the family endured. Geraldine and her mother somehow convinced Eustis's parents that bringing Hamilton to the United States gave him more opportunities, especially in education. Eustis and his parents agreed, as they knew of the enormous benefits of the American educational system, which was more than would be offered to Hamilton in Jamaica, regardless of the family's status.

Geraldine's family secured documents for her and Hamilton to travel to Charm Town. He cried every day for two weeks and he never saw or spoke to his father or his grandparents again. After years of asking his mother of his sudden departure from his father and not getting an answer, he gave up asking the questions. He was certain his mother harbored regrets about his departure from Jamaica, but never spoke of them. Years later, as an adult, he found out when his mother learned she had family living in the United States, she decided to leave Jamaica and move with her young son in hopes of carving out a better life for them. However, it bothered, and sometimes angered, Hamilton that his father or his family never looked for him, sent a note, or attempted to contact him. He vowed to be a better father if given the opportunity.

The move to Charm Town was good for Geraldine. She obtained her General Equivalency Diploma and bachelor degree in nursing from Coppin State College. Hamilton remembered his mother cried the day she received her nursing certification and job offer from Charm Town General Hospital in the pediatrics department. Geraldine remained at Charm Town General for the duration of her career and retired as a head nurse. Never married, she devoted her time to raising Hamilton. She ensured his acceptance at his school and in his social circles.

She pretended to feel comfortable around the predominantly white, rich parents of his friends. Most of them knew nothing of Jamaica or its people, except for the little they read in books and saw on television or in the movies. Occasionally, someone got the courage to ask about her hair or the texture of her skin, and she always found a polite way to answer and never revealed her offended feelings. She and Hamilton talked about her childhood and the challenges of growing up poor. Education was her passion and she believed life was hard without a good education, particularly for someone of Jamaican descent. She spent the remainder of her earthly time with friends, church, and charity work. She died in Hamilton's arms at the age of seventy-three of natural causes.

In Charm Town, Geraldine's family was admired for their generosity toward the less fortunate, and well known for their long business history of drug trafficking and distribution. Her brother, Lester, the mastermind, started out on the corners of Wabash and Liberty selling dope. Uncle Lester, the name Hamilton called him, rose to drug prominence in the community of Windsor Heights. He made friends with law enforcement officials and politicians with his easy style, permanent smile, and refusal to leave bodies in abandoned houses and in streets over small, petty arguments. Uncle Lester believed the young drug boys messed up a perfectly fine drug game when they shot people over dumb matters. He knew bodies brought the police, the FBI and, in some cases, the CIA. Dead bodies all over town were a sure way for a drug boy's game to abruptly end. He also knew the drug game was a short-lived one, with a strong chance of death or life imprisonment. Uncle Lester was fortunate to enjoy what most in the game didn't—a long livelihood.

His annual Easter and Thanksgiving food basket giveaways to the poor were legendary. He padded the pockets of influential individuals with cash and enjoyed unprecedented protection. Charged several times with drug crimes that carried harsh penalties, he avoided conviction by a jury. Although he cultivated some enemies in his time, his money was too generous and too long. Charm Town had a long history of juries that didn't convict for drug charges. It was a known fact that many town residents believed folk were frequently "setup" to be arrested and sent to prison. It was their way of fighting the so-called conspiracy and all those elected officials who talked tough on combating drugs and, at the same time, enjoyed their private parties where cocaine and heroin were appetizers of choice. Coincidentally, those drugs were from the same streets of the kingpins they attempted to convict.

Uncle Lester was smart. He invested money in legitimate enterprises, such as real estate and a Jamaican restaurant, The Montegan, the first of its kind in Charm Town. He also invested in Hamilton's education and paid his tuition to attend the very prestigious Gilman School for Boys. At Gilman, Hamilton learned about the benefits of wealth, having the privilege of befriending some very rich kids. He enjoyed vacations to foreign countries and ski trips to some of the best resorts in America and abroad. Introduced to the sport of ice hockey at Gilman, the parents of his teammates and opponents were amazed at his skills in a sport largely unknown to Black youth.

Childhood for Hamilton was fun and full of things young boys liked to do when they didn't have to worry about money, the lights being turned off, no food in the refrigerator, or getting set out on the street for nonpayment of rent. The only Black and Jamaican kid in his school, he was one of the popular kids in his class, in large part because most of his classmates were curious about him. They wondered about the dark, carefree, laid-back, always polite, cute kid with the million-dollar smile who dressed in all the latest designer clothes and sometimes had a driver pick him up from his home in the Beverly Hills neighborhood on the northeast side of town and bring him to and from school. Always invited to birthday parties, sleepovers, bar and bat mitzvahs, spring break, and summer trips, he was popular with the girls, too, who wanted to be around him. Several called themselves "Hamilton chicks" and attended most of his sports games to cheer for him.

Hamilton's one girlfriend in high school, Emily Goldberg, was from a nice, liberal, wealthy, Jewish family that lived in Ruxton Hills. She was educated across from him at The Bryn Mawr School for Girls. They dated their sophomore through senior years, and she was the first person with whom he enjoyed a sexual relationship. He thought her parents and his folks would kill him for having the balls to sex a white girl, but no one seemed to care. It happened the way they planned it. Emily invited Hamilton to join her family at their beach home in Bethany. One night, her parents went to dinner with friends and left them alone with burgers and soda. She started playing the music of her favorite bands, Journey and Foreigner, and the next thing he knew, she took off her top and bra, and asked him if he liked what he saw. Hamilton was speechless, but never resisted. Nervous, but afraid to disappoint, he allowed Emily to take the lead. She didn't disappoint and she enjoyed her first sexual experience. From that day forward, they enjoyed sex whenever they devised a story to stay away alone together.

Emily's parents were education attorneys who worked mainly on issues of race and its affect upon poor children. Hamilton stayed in their home often and listened to her parents share tales of the American education system and the biases toward minority and poor kids. They often spoke of the codes and the connection to government funding streams for education in poor communities. They loved him, not judging because of his race, but liking him because of his character and personality. Emily liked Hamilton because everyone liked him and wanted to be around him. He was genuinely nice and good at most things he did. He liked her because she was pretty, popular and liked everything about him. They talked and laughed on the phone at night about the stares they got from both black and white people. Sometimes, they purposely kissed, hugged, and held hands in public to see the reactions from folks on the street. Neither understood why their relationship created discomfort and anger among some people.

Emily's parents were saddened when the two broke up the summer of graduation. Hamilton left town to attend Morehouse College in Atlanta and Emily left to attend Syracuse University in New York. Their friendship lasted into their adult years, with each checking on the other long after they both married and had children. Occasionally, they met for lunch when the other happened to be in town on business. Emily's husband, Neil Weissman, was never a fan of her relationship with Hamilton and often complained of it. He couldn't understand how a Jewish girl from an affluent family connected with a Black, Jamaican kid from a family no one knew much about. His family and friends often taunted and teased that his wife would leave him for a Jamaican. Unfazed by Neil's insecurities, Emily enjoyed her lasting bond and admiration for Hamilton. Hamilton's friends and their parents frequented The Montegan and talked with Uncle Lester for hours about how he got started in the restaurant business. They were curious about the Jamaican culture and Uncle Lester was always willing to educate them on the *truths* of Jamaica and its people, dispelling the horrible myths that American culture perpetuated. Hamilton doubted any of them ever knew about Uncle Lester's *other* business and Uncle Lester made sure those *other* friends weren't hanging around the restaurant when Hamilton's friends' parents visited. Once, the dad of one of his friends hosted a bachelor party at The Montegan. It was the first time Hamilton saw strippers. What surprised him was these white men didn't want white strippers. They specifically requested Uncle Lester's place because they wanted Black strippers and knew he would be able to provide them and be discreet about their wishes. It was Hamilton's first introduction to white men's sexual interest in Black women. He was fifteen years old and shocked at the revelation.

Hamilton enjoyed his relationship with Uncle Lester, who served as a father figure. They went to ball games, annual camping trips, talked long hours about Jamaica and frequented exclusive restaurants in Charm Town. As a child, he never knew how his mother's brother obtained his fortune, but was sure the profits from The Montegan didn't solely sustain his ability to provide for himself and some of Geraldine and Hamilton's expenses. It was during his sophomore year at Morehouse when he learned the truth. By then, Uncle Lester was in his later years and in declining health. He died of a massive stroke during Hamilton's senior year of college. Fortunate for him, his uncle paid the remainder of his college tuition, car payment, and apartment rent for a year after his scheduled graduation date. In addition, Uncle Lester left his trunks of cash and expensive cars to his sister Geraldine and a legacy of goodwill and good friends who looked out for Hamilton and helped him start his business career upon his return home after his time in college.

Hamilton chose to start his professional career in Charm Town, despite lucrative job offers from top rated corporations in Miami, New York, Chicago, Dallas, Los Angeles, and Seattle. His first position after college was in the hospitality industry. He met Sandra, his future wife, when he worked as a restaurant manager for Gertrude's Bistro, while she worked as a hostess for Hot Tomatoes restaurant. It was a cold afternoon at the Restaurant Depot when Hamilton went there to check on some orders and Sandra was there with her boss as part of the training for her position. He instantly noticed her presence and she instantly noticed his good looks. She was a tall, light-skinned, and striking young woman who didn't initially give in to his advances. It was only after several dates that she began to feel she might like him. After dating for two years, they married in a small church on the south side of Charm Town. The first two years were incredible, full of many laughs, vacations, dinners, and time alone together. Once the children were born, their relationship suffered and it was during their fifth year of marriage that he began his first affair. His lover was an impressionable, beautiful, young woman in Charm Town completing a medical internship with John Memorial Hospital. She studied oncology and wasn't looking for much from Hamilton or demanding of his time. He enjoyed spending time with her because she challenged the way he thought about things. Next was a continual stream of women whom he never fully developed connections. Careful not to demean any of his acquaintances, he never met a woman who captured his full attention and devotion, mainly because he knew she was aware of his financial situation and family reputation and was happy to experience the good life with him for a time.

Due to the complexity of his and Sandra's business relationship and ownership interests, divorce didn't seem a viable option for Hamilton. His mistresses did not pressure him to leave her and he was sure she had an idea of his liaisons. He appreciated she never directly confronted him with the prospect of divorce. He wouldn't have known what to say because, frankly, he didn't know himself why he needed the attention of multiple women. Never rude, disrespectful or violent, but attentive, accommodating and loving toward his companions, his relationships tended to end with amicable departures and the women speaking of him in friendly terms. He, however, did know that he and Sandra connected in ways not many others knew or understood.

Sandra Banks came from a rich family and grew up in the exclusive Washington Hill community of Charm Town. Well-bred, driven, and articulate, she attended Charm Town Public Schools and college in Charm Town at Morgan State University. She enjoyed a superior childhood, full of spoils from her parents. She, too, was a member of the exclusive Jack and Jill of America organization and participated in most of the elite activities for young Black children in her community, partaking in her first cotillion at age fifteen. Known for her superb intelligence, she was a popular person in high school and college, and in her young adult years was always on invite lists of the "in events" of fraternal organizations, political groups, and corporate groups. Dating wasn't a challenge for her. Attracted to men who willingly fulfilled her desires, she enjoyed one-sided relationships, as well as lasting friendships with a core group of girlfriends she traveled with and shared birthdays, weddings, baby showers, and a few funerals. Sometimes edgy and unpredictable, she enjoyed working as a restaurant host for recreational money. She understood the unspoken pressure of her family to continue the perception that money was endless because she came from a family of generations of wealth.

Sandra endured one major mishap in her young life: an unplanned, unwanted pregnancy that she ended almost as soon as she found out. As a young graduate student, she attended an educational conference at the invitation of one of her professors. At the conference, she met a good-looking, fast-talking man who swept her off her feet and invited her to share drinks and dinner with him each night. He was a young, college professor who presented a research paper he wrote on the effects of socio-economic status on the education system. After several nights of cocktails, an affair ensued. At the end of the conference, both decided to return to their separate lives and remember their time together as something spontaneous to share with their grandchildren. When she found out she was pregnant, the decision to abort the child was easy for her. She chose not to contact the father, knowing he would most likely reject her, given their understanding when they parted ways. She also knew she wasn't ready for parenthood or the reactions from her family and friends. She was ashamed and embarrassed to disclose her actions and mistake. Sandra knew she couldn't withstand the disappointment of her parents if they found out she compromised her professional career. Her decision was quick and the action quicker, with Sandra utilizing a fictitious name at the clinic, further concealing her secret. She couldn't risk name recognition and subjecting her family to judgment and ridicule. She never spoke to anyone about this event in her life, although part of her continued to carry regret and remorse for her decision and action. When Hamilton suggested she consider abortion when she became pregnant with their third child, she cursed him. Shocked at her angry response, he agreed with her decision to carry the child. Unfortunately, she suffered a miscarriage early in the pregnancy. Hamilton appeared devastated, but Sandra knew he was relieved about the ending.

Her passion was teaching, as her first job in education was a teacher in the Charm Town school district. A dedicated advocate for children, she rose to lead teacher, department head, assistant principal, principal, school board member, and president of the school board. She oftentimes expressed to Hamilton her frustration at the number of children she saw standing on the street corners of Charm Town, obviously with no meaningful place to go. No matter the time of day, there were also scores of men, —Black, young, and old—who stood on many corners of the town. They displayed a look of defeat on their faces, as if they knew time and life were passing by them. She felt the school system, on some level, failed those individuals, and wanted to make a difference. She was a strong believer in education being the gas needed to drive the car of hope and prosperity. For some reason, those individuals never realized the opportunities of education while most were engaged in the Charm Town School District.

Married for twenty-one years, Sandra and Hamilton had two children: Maysa, sixteen years old, and Dustin, fourteen years old. To Sandra, it mainly was a happy marriage, although she secretly held contempt toward Hamilton because of his philandering ways. She was not accustomed to such treatment from her man. She became aware of his affair with a medical student after being married for five years. When confronted about the affair, Hamilton begged her to forgive him and stay, promising a change in his behavior. She agreed and their relationship improved temporarily. Within a year, he entangled himself in another extramarital situation and enjoyed multiple affairs over the years. He thought she was unaware of those relations, that she was the naive wife who believed everything her husband told her. Despite the infidelity, they built a mini empire together, acquiring real estate holdings, stocks, and silent interests in a variety of enterprises. The money from Uncle Lester's last will and testament served them well.

Sandra was not sure what she was going to do about Hamilton's liaisons. She knew her actions had to be careful and calculated. She thought she should get herself involved in her own affair and forget about his indiscretions. It's not as if men never approached her. The Charm Town School police chief continuously rang her phone with excuses, many unrelated to police work, to talk and meet with her. First, it was to speak about the rising number of students arrested during school hours, the rise and fall in standardized test scores, the student who was a life-long Charm Town schools student and accepted to all the major ivy league colleges on full scholarship, the uncovering of the teacher who created a credit card fraud scheme on school property, the students who were chosen to study in Africa in a foreign exchange program, the former student from the school of design who recently married a popular actor, the student who openly practiced an alternative religion, the teacher who was accused of having an affair with some of the athletes on the softball team, and the custodians who crafted an elaborate theft scheme in several of the elementary schools, stealing new computer equipment and selling them on the internet. When those issues didn't work, he wanted to discuss how the school district and school police could collaborate on combating the drug issue in schools. It never ended and she wasn't interested in him, although the attention was flattering. She only accepted his calls and responded to his emails because of her position with the district. She knew he had a fiancée for the third time and a history of domestic battery troubles. She decided she didn't need to be involved with that kind of hassle or attention. Then there was the president of Truth State College who constantly questioned her marital happiness and propositioned her at a school meeting last spring, inviting her to dinner and drinks. They had dinner, but no love affair ensued. His arrogance and cockiness were annoying and offensive. He kept commenting about how women couldn't keep their hands off him and his dick. That was the last of the pursuits she considered. A divorce would disrupt everything that was in place. She hoped Hamilton felt the same.

Chapter Three

I t was a normal, hot, sunny, summer afternoon, barely any breeze, and there hadn't been rain for more than a week. The day was calm, no breaking news stories and downtown bustled with tourists visiting museums, heading to the ballgame and savoring some of the flavors of the local cafes and bistros. Traffic flowed well as they rode on the streets of Charm Town, air-conditioning blasting, waving to the cute construction workers with sweat covering their faces, and singing along to the latest tunes of Adele and Alicia Keys. It was an exciting and relaxing summer of dating, trips to the Caribbean, drinks on the yacht at the marina and late night grill parties. "Gina, why don't you park on the corner over there and I'll run in and grab it. I hope leaving out of the building without signing out is worth it. You know some of those nosy ass people in that building are always looking for us for some dumb reason and trying to determine where we are, and what we're doing, and I know that damn SAP coordinator will be calling the main office, saying she doesn't know where I am. She really needs to get a life or better yet, get a man. I swear I don't think that woman has gotten laid in years and if she has it sure as hell couldn't have been good."

Gina continued driving, bobbing her head to the music, barely listening to what was said.

Peyton repeatedly snapped her fingers in her direction hoping to gain her attention.

"You always get me in some shit and I always go for it. Now, here we are running across town, chasing down some fucking bread pudding. What the hell? Who even eats bread pudding anymore? It's something my grandma used to make and she's been dead for years. You've been talking about this damn apple cinnamon bread pudding since beginning of summer and we're now back to work with two days before the start of school and you want to come get some goddamn bread pudding? All I can say is it better be good because I got a shitload of work to do before the kids show up." She rambled on, conscious and annoyed that her bestie was still absorbed in the music.

Gina pulled over to the curb, brought her shiny new car to a stop, and turned down the radio's volume.

"Just hurry up Peyton," she said in her notorious I'm annoyed tone. "You're right; people will probably be looking for us, but who cares? You know how many teachers and school folk leave the building every day and *never* sign out? I'm still feeling like summer break hasn't ended and today I just happen to have a sweet tooth and our next meeting isn't until later this afternoon. Principal Jackson is probably going to be wondering where I am if we're gone too long, so I guess we shouldn't stop by Elite Secrets on North Charles to check out the latest designs by Khemistry. We're only at the beginning of the school year and he acts as if he can't operate that damn Alternative Ed department without me. Everyone knows the beginning of the year is crazy in that department with all those confidential binders coming in from other schools. He's the one with the doctorate degree that he never lets anyone forget about, so let him figure it out. Maybe I should have fucked him. Maybe that would have calmed his ass down a little."

Peyton looked at Gina with an exasperated expression, rolled her eyes, and shook her head.

"Can you try and have a conversation without mentioning fucking or any derivative of it?"

Gina Carey was the sensually attractive, always talkative, superbly dressed, and charismatic assistant principal of Alternative Education Services for Montebello High School. A spicy personality, she had no problem telling folks exactly what she thought. Peyton loved Gina and quickly became friends with her when she came to Montebello five years ago, after a transfer from another high school that closed due to low student attendance and state assessment scores. Gina approached her on day one, introduced herself, and asked if she needed assistance with her transition to the school. Peyton appreciated her genuineness. It was refreshing because she was familiar with Black women who took pride in stabbing other Black women in the back. She never understood the underlying hatred and vile that some Black women held toward each other for no apparent reason. Being an attractive Black woman and having to work for another Black woman who may not feel as attractive was sometimes hell on earth. She remembered Paula Jennings and Tot Golding, two older, Black women who needed to retire and get a fulfilling life. They were administrators in the district who did everything in their leadership role to make her time at their schools miserable from day one. When she complained of sexual harassment at Paula Jennings's school, administration dismissed her complaints and accused Peyton of drawing attention by wearing designer, expensive clothes, and did nothing to ease her concerns.

A Charm Town native, Gina received her undergraduate degree in education from Bennett College and joined the school district after receiving her Master's Degree in Education from Spelman College. She grew tired of working in affluent, predominantly Caucasian communities and decided to return to her hometown and help the young people from her childhood community and beyond. She was married to Bert Carey, an owner of a chain of auto mechanic shops and they shared one child. Although married, Gina enjoyed her share of extramarital affairs. She grew weary of her husband of fifteen years and his endless list of problems he couldn't seem to solve. She always said she needed an outlet, which turned out to be male companionship. Her selection of companions usually involved individuals who worked in professions other than education, although there were occasions when she violated her own policy of never engaging in intimate, sexual relationships with colleagues. Once, Gina found herself in the bed of the director of the school district's tax services, Dexter Warren, a single father of a very troubled and promiscuous teenage daughter who had him wrapped around her finger. The two were former high school classmates at Carroll Park. Dexter spent a better part of a year making flirtatious comments to Gina and flat out invited her to join him for a weekend getaway at Deep Creek Lake, promising her the best sex ever. "That's the first sign of terrible sex, when the guy makes all these promises of how good it's *going to* be," she said when she recounted the weekend with Peyton at Donna's Coffeehouse.

She happily joined him for a weekend, and enjoyed luxury accommodations, spa treatments, expensive wine, and exquisite cuisine. He took her shopping, and treated her to all her personal delights at *Lush*, her favorite soap store. According to Gina, all was great until it came to the sex part and she was blunt.

"He was horrendous and I *almost* felt sorry for his ass." Peyton almost spat out her chai tea latte as Gina continued.

"I was just lying there thinking, I can't believe I'm going to have to fake this shit at least two or three more times. He is having all kinds of trouble just getting it up."

Peyton's laughter drew attention from a few patrons as Gina continued with her animation.

"You know as well as I P that there is nothing worse than having pretend sex with somebody who thinks they are God's gift to women. I just wanted to tell his fake-ass, wannabe lover self to take me the hell home. He talked all that shit and in the end, didn't have shit. I was pissed that he wasted my fuckin' time and left my ass horny. I had to come home and call another one of my side dicks to accommodate my needs."

That was the end of the Gina and Dexter tryst and they continued to see each other at work events and acted as if nothing happened. Gina never told him her true feelings, only that she felt guilt for cheating on her husband. She was a good liar at times.

Peyton again rolled her eyes at her friend as she grabbed her newly purchased Louis Vuitton bag and exited the vehicle. She carefully crossed the street and made her way to the corner restaurant at Whitmore and Eden Streets. She never noticed the place before and drove past this corner many times, usually on her way to a home visit for one of her students. As she approached the door, it appeared dark inside.

Damn, I hope they aren't closed. This would just be our luck and Gina never confirms times for anything.

Peyton tugged on the door and it opened with ease.

Yes, thank goodness they are open.

She breathed deeply and walked into a space of inviting aromas and lively conversation.

The Lucky Café sat conspicuously at the corner of the busy streets. The top-selling, national magazine *Ebony* featured the establishment in its special summer edition. It was a frequent feature of the local 6:00 news and the Charm Town Magazine.

A trendy eatery, it consistently received positive patron reviews and remained on the exclusive list of Charm Town's favorite food spots. Cars raced by and slowed as the curious leaned out their window to snap a picture. Extremely popular and a one-of-a-kind restaurant, The Lucky Café maintained a wait list for dinner most evenings and always for its weekend brunch. Frequented by business folk, regular folk, media personalities, political figures, and some high profile members of the Charm Town sports teams, it was likened to First Avenue in Minneapolis or BB King's Blues Club in Memphis. It was the place to be, and most visited by celebrities when in town for movie shoots and music concerts. Business deals, reputations, careers, affairs, engagements, and breakups launched or ended at the Lucky Café.

Peyton walked inside, and immediately noticed the layout of the space. There were two-top, four-top, and six-top tables in a strategically arranged area with an open kitchen design. A sign indicated a private dining area, but she saw none. Storage shelves and freezers were visible farther in the back. There was a plasma television attached to the wall stationed on MSNBC live with Tamron Hall with the volume muted and pop music played softly in the background. She eyed what looked like reviews from the *Charm Town Times* newspaper and other local publications framed and hung on one wall, with exotic looking pieces of artwork on all the other walls. There were two electronic boards situated on opposite sides of the room listing the food menu and daily chef specials. A young man who looked of Latino descent cleaned at one of the visible stoves. She imagined the place sat at least one hundred fifty patrons.

Peyton decided there was no time to study the menu. After all, she was merely there to pick up two pieces of this bread pudding her best friend, Gina, would not shut up about, who visited the Lucky Café with her new man on the side, Walter, for dinner one hot evening a few weeks ago and sampled the bread pudding dessert, among other things that night. She talked nonstop about the incredible sex and bread pudding ever since that date.

Peyton made her way to what looked like the carryout counter, passed the empty host stand, and observed the patrons seated in the room that remained after the lunch hour.

"May I assist you?" asked the calm, yet deliberate, deep voice coming from behind her.

She spun to see him sitting at one of the two-top tables with a young girl who she decided was either an employee or family member.

She looks too young to be a girlfriend, but then again some of these guys like the young ones.

He was a breathtakingly beautiful, dark chocolate-hued, dark-eyed, well-groomed man with a perfectly sculpted goatee that was insanely perfect for his perfect face. There was not a scar or pimple visible to the eye. He had close cut, dark black hair. His skin was smooth, even, and gave the impression of velvet. He looked as sweet as a piece of Hershey's special dark chocolate candy. He sat slightly slouched in the chair, and looked up into Peyton's face. She wished she could read what his stare said because hers said, *Holy cow; he is one sexy man.*

She instantaneously felt her body break into a sweat and she knew the feeling well. She last experienced it with Maury, a Los Angeles based pediatrician she met while visiting New Orleans. Her relationship with him was passionate, intense and ended badly. For some reason, Maury still felt the need to phone whenever he would be near town, but Peyton never caved to his requests for sex. She was all for good sex, but his always came with some crazy condition or two that she didn't wish to entertain. He never seemed to find the time to call or text her to say hello. She surmised he hadn't gotten the unwritten memo that it costs to play.

Conscious of her immediate attraction to him, she noticed a simple silver band on his left ring finger. Ignoring that factor in her thoughts, she wondered what he was like in the sheets, what it would be like to have sex with him.

Hmmm, I wonder what it would be like to feel all that chocolate inside me.

"Hi, yes. Uh, I'd like to pick up two pieces of your apple cinnamon bread pudding please. My best friend, Gina, tells me there's no better bread pudding in town and she's out in the car and she dragged me over here to get some. We're supposed to be at work at our school. We both work for the school system. She's an assistant principal and I'm a social worker." Peyton couldn't believe how she babbled like an attention-seeking eight-year-old.

What is your problem? Is all that information necessary for bread pudding?

"Absolutely, let me get that for you," Hershey's special dark chocolate let flow confidently out of his beautiful lips, as he stood up, revealed a svelte, six-foot-two-inch lean, tight frame and walked behind the counter. Peyton could immediately tell by the way his T-shirt and shorts hung on his body that he exercised regularly. She spotted the Sean John logo on his underwear peeking out from under the back of his black shorts. His arms were in exact proportion to his body and his torso supremely complemented his lower frame. She suddenly felt this would be no ordinary purchase because this man didn't appear to be an ordinary man.

"Thanks, and did I mention I need that to go?" she asked and, for a nanosecond, felt guilty about not caring if this man was married or otherwise involved. There was something different about this one. In her short time in the Lucky Café, she wanted to know him and his story. She knew she would have to return because Gina was outside and would soon begin honking the horn if she didn't hurry back to the car. Suddenly, people at Montebello looking for them were no concern for her.

"No, ma'am, and that's not a problem. Is this your first time here?"

Peyton's grin was wide. "Yes, it is and it's a really nice place."

Keep calm, just keep calm, and stop grinning in his face.

"Okay, I'm happy to help you and welcome to The Lucky Café where in here, we believe all our patrons are recipients of some kind of good luck. I was just helping my daughter, Maysa, with her calculus work."

He was exquisite, not like men she generally saw around town. She tried not to stare and instead began looking at the paper menus and business cards situated at the front counter. Over the top of the menu, she stole glimpses of him as he navigated around the front space, grabbing two to go containers, a bag, and a knife to cut the dessert item. He moved with ease and a smoothness that, to her, communicated sexual confidence.

Damn, I have not seen anyone this fine in a long time. Where has he been hiding? Right here in Charm Town?

He exuded comfort and peace in his environment and Peyton, again, became conscious of her body sweating, particularly her armpits. She looked down to remind herself which blouse she wore. She hoped it didn't reveal any perspiration stains.

How embarrassed will I be in front of this gorgeous man, who clearly is in his element and cool as a cucumber?

After what seemed two seconds, he was back at the counter with her bag. "Anything else ma'am?" he asked in a sultry voice.

You don't want to know, you really don't want to know.

"No thanks, that's it. How much do I owe?"

"Nine-fifty please."

"So, are you the proprietor of this place?" she asked, as she handed him a ten-dollar bill. "Keep the change."

"Thank you, and yes, I am the owner. My name is Hamilton Banks and thank you for visiting my establishment today."

Hamilton Banks. That name has a nice ring to it.

Peyton became intent on learning his personal story.

Are you married, and if so, what does she do? Do you have any other children? Are you from Charm Town? What do you do when you are not here? Do all the women who come in here get excited over you as I am?

"Good to meet you Mr. Banks and thank you," she said, as she took the bag from his hand. "I'll have to come back soon."

"Well I hope you will, Ms.?"

"Oh, it's Peyton, Peyton Stanfield."

"Hello, Peyton Stanfield." He extended his hand to shake hers. It was smooth.

"Pleased to meet you and I look forward to welcoming you back to the café soon." He never looked beyond her face. She wondered if he used his eyes to purposely entice or communicate something to her.

"Thank you," Peyton muttered, as she turned to walk out the door. She hoped he hadn't noticed the armpit stains on her blouse. Thank God, he was unable to see that her panties were moist. She again noticed the young girl, his daughter, still sitting at the table. She smiled at her, as she made her way to the exit.

Once outside the door, Peyton glanced back and Hamilton stared directly at her. Nervous and body temperature rising more, she immediately turned away, looked in both directions of Whitmore Street and almost sprinted to Gina's Volvo sedan. She bought the car with money she received from Principal Graham at Hillside High School for an indiscretion some years ago. Their affair yielded a lucrative payday for Gina. She received a significant monetary incentive to remain silent and agree to a school transfer. That was during the days when principals wrote checks from school bank accounts with little accountability. The night custodian spotted her and Principal Graham engaged in a sex act in his car in the school garage. The custodian initially agreed to discretion, but somehow the story leaked among the teachers and students. It became an unproductive work environment for Gina and at the request of Principal Graham, she received a friendly transfer to a new school. Most women would have been humiliated and embarrassed, but not Gina. She welcomed the transfer and looked forward to new experiences at a new school. That's the type of woman she was, never saw the bad in a situation, only what she could benefit from it. Principal Graham managed to survive the talk, but received a stern reprimand from his supervisor at school headquarters. He has remained the principal of Hillside. Peyton heard he was involved in another incident, an untimely pregnancy of one of his teachers who filed a paternity suit against him. It was scandalous because Principal Graham was married.

Peyton quickly opened the car door, hopped inside, settled in the seat, closed her eyes, and gasped for air.

Gina looked at her with a perplexed glare and turned down the music of her favorite Rhythm and Blues artist Maxwell.

"What the hell is wrong with you?" She paused. "You got the bread budding?" she asked matter-of-factly, grabbing the bag from Peyton's lap. "I hope you didn't forget the forks and is it hot? I want mine *right* now."

"Girl, there is enough heat with the man in that place for this bread pudding and anything else you might need warmed up. Have you met the owner of this place? Why didn't you warn me before I went in there of how *good looking* he is?" Peyton ignored Gina's questions, her eyes tightly closed. She relished in her mental pictorial of Hamilton.

"No, not personally. When I was here, it was all about Walter and his gigantic dick. However, I do know he is supposedly a hotshot business guy who has plenty of money. The night we were here, he was walking around, smiling, and greeting each table. Walter knew of him, saying he comes from a family who made their fortune in questionable ways, if you get my drift."

Peyton again ignored Gina and spoke in a confident voice as if she had known Hamilton for years.

"He's Hamilton Banks and as soon as I laid eyes on his ass, I got excited and that hasn't happened to me in years. Do you hear me? That's years, I said. I don't know, Gina. I'm feeling something different about that interaction. I don't know what it is, but I'm feeling something different, some sort of connection to that man. He reminds me of Idris Elba or Mike Colter with his smooth chocolate skin, beautiful set of teeth, hot body, and cool, calm voice. I nearly wet my pants looking at him. Actually my drawers are wet, and look at my armpits." Peyton raised her left arm to reveal the perspiration stains.

"He is fine as all fine can be," she continued, "but I'm sure he probably has tons of game with him. Oh, and I think he's married because I saw what looked like a wedding band on his ring finger. He definitely has at least one child and his daughter is in there with him now. She looked a little bratty to me, eying me as if to tell me, *don't even think about getting with my dad* as I was walking out."

"And you care about all that because? Who gives a shit about the wedding band, bratty kid, or kids? The wife is probably somewhere doing her own thing. You know that's how it goes nowadays. What went on in there? You sure did get a lot of info in a short period of time." Gina spoke and eyed Peyton with a raised brow.

"Nothing yet, but I'll be back," Peyton said as she glanced at The Lucky Café as Gina sped off, turned up the music and headed back to Montebello. "Yes, Mr. Hamilton Banks, as sure as the sun rises and sets, I *will* be back."

Chapter Four

The first day of school at Montebello Senior High School was no different from the first day at most Charm Town schools—painted building, walls scrubbed, floors waxed, bathrooms cleaned with stalls stocked with paper and soap. The outside lot was full of cars: teachers looking for parking, parents dropping off their children, a few kids who were lucky to have a car and school police who felt it necessary to have a strong presence on the first day. While appreciated, they always parked their cars in places that blocked the easy movements of others. It was no secret some of them thought they could do whatever they wanted, including parking their raggedy, dirty cars on grassy areas, sidewalks, and in the way of moving traffic. No one made much fuss about it because most of the officers, even with an air of badge entitlement, were friendly and helped whenever and wherever needed on school grounds.

Veteran teachers reported early and made last minute preparations in their classrooms, while new teachers nervously moved about their rooms, unsure of the responses they would give or receive from the children on their roster. The young, immature, and animated students streamed in through the front door dressed in new, crisp uniform shirts and pants. Their faces were bright-eyed and ready for whatever came their way. The boys donned fresh haircuts and the girls showed off newly sewn-in, colored weaves. Some of the students came because they were ready and eager to begin classes, while some came because they wanted to escape the unhappiness, drama, or pain of their homes and the boredom of summer. There weren't many organized, safe, relevant, and free activities for poor kids during the summer. Not all the students reported the first day, a norm for Charm Town schools. Some didn't come until the following week because there wasn't money until after the first of the month, when the child services check arrived, to purchase the required clothing items. Montebello offered new and used uniforms at a discount, but they were few in number. Occasionally, there were some uniforms made available at no cost to the student, but never enough for the numbers needed. Peyton wondered why the school board hadn't returned the start date to after the Labor Day holiday, as it was in previous years. She accepted her position as school social worker because she wanted to help children and families get a good education that would improve their lives. With all the uncertainty of the system, she still believed in the children and families of the town and felt they deserved better than they sometimes received. *Why can't Charm Town kids have the same access to equipment, materials, facilities, and support as their peers in the affluent school districts? It just doesn't seem fair that all kids, no matter the district, are evaluated in the same manner and take the same assessments, but have widely different access to resources.*

Montebello was a Title A school, which meant a majority of its families' incomes and financial resources were limited. It sat in a community of Charm Town that was home to a world-renowned poet, beautiful, vacant, three-story, architecturally sound brownstones and some of the most dedicated teachers in the district. It was also known for crime, unemployment, and broken families. The kind of community that future politicians visited when campaigning for office to make all sorts of promises for a better life only to forget about those promises when elected. Montebello was also a school in need of serious physical repair. Teachers and students described the exterior of the building as resemblance to a prison house because of the small windows and bars placed across the doorways. Constructed in the late 1960's, with minimal renovations made since that time, the building boasted narrow hallways and stairwells and no central air-conditioning. Gang-related graffiti, testimonials to deceased classmates, and confessions of love between students adorned the walls. The cafeteria housed the picnic style tables that were uncomfortable for some of the smallest and largest students. In the winter, students and teachers complained of being cold because the heating unit malfunctioned, and the windows had no insulation and no longer closed properly. There was also the ever-presence of mice running down the hallways during the day and leaving droppings in the classrooms overnight. Occasionally, the custodians laid traps and caught a few overnight, only for the teachers and students to find upon their return the next day.

Montebello had a number of talented and bright students who understood and valued the importance of an education. A fair number managed to graduate each year and gained acceptance into two and four-year colleges, trade institutions, the military and specialized internships. Those students reported to class, turned in homework, asked for extra credit, stayed after school for teacher assistance, joined a club or sport, and spent time with the guidance counselor researching career, school, and scholarship options. Most of their parents participated in school-related activities, flashed proud smiles, and held on to the high hope that their child would somehow make it to college. The school also had a number of struggling students, and students who dropped out of school and allowed to return to obtain their diploma. Those were the students who skipped school, hooked class for hallway crap games, were suspended, chose street life over school, endured serious emotional and behavior problems and self-medicated with high-risk behaviors, pills, weed, cigarettes, and alcohol. A number had high levels of lead from childhood in their bodies, were born to substance-addicted mothers, or endured severe early childhood trauma, which accounted for some of the school troubles. Most of their parents were unreachable and almost never engaged in school-related functions. These parents only showed up and showed out if their child reported a teacher hit or disrespected them. Some of these students ended up incarcerated, sworn to street life, or murdered.

Teachers at Montebello were highly qualified and experienced, dedicated to their craft and committed to the students. Many held teaching degrees from well-respected institutions, namely Teachers College, Tuskegee University, Bowdoin College, Dartmouth College, and Howard University. Many willingly worked long hours, after school and on weekends, helped their students get extra assistance with academics or organized some new project or learning opportunity. They believed all students, regardless of circumstance, deserved the opportunity to learn and better themselves. Many used personal funds, rarely reimbursed, to purchase class supplies, additional learning tools, food, and personal items for students who didn't have them at their home.

The school's principal, Cecil Jackson, a ruggedly handsome, caramel-hued man, dressed in a baby blue, button-down, Bloomingdales shirt with Montebello embroidered on the left top corner and khaki slacks, stood at the front door and greeted staff, students, and parents to another school year. He was cleanly shaven and his head was a shining bald. He was a very good-looking man.

"Good morning, Mr. Jackson," Peyton mouthed, as she struggled past the long line of students awaiting their turn at the metal detector before entering the building and running to get class schedules. She noticed two of the school police officers busy checking bags for anything inappropriate for the school setting, like weapons, cigarettes, alcohol, or drugs. Peyton rolled her eyes at this because she knew it was something only done on the first several days of school, or when the school was on high alert. She and the teachers in the building strongly believed in daily, year-round inspection of bags, especially since the incident when there was a student stabbed to death in the school cafeteria in a neighboring school district. Apparently, two female students fought each other for years and no one seemed to know what started the beef between them. One day, it all culminated when the ninth-grade student walked into the school's cafeteria, during the crowded lunch hour, and stabbed her nemesis, permanently paralyzing an eleventh-grade student. After the young girl's arrest, the court deemed her unfit to stand trial, and remanded her to a psychiatric hospital. Peyton was friends with the social worker at their school, who told her when the suspension meeting happened with the parents of the two girls, a family member revealed they were related, cousins, she thought. Their story and the subject of school safety was a hot topic and in the news for weeks. Although the incident didn't happen in Charm Town, Peyton was aware of many incidents of students bringing weapons to Montebello to threaten others or for protection. The consequences of their actions were lost to the idea of victimization. For the students, self-protection was critical in the environment in which they lived, sometimes meaning a matter of life or death. Some acknowledged bringing knives, blades, hammers and guns for protection from troubles on the streets while in transit to and from school. Gang activity among young people was alive in certain areas of Charm Town.

"Hey Ms. Stanfield, Good Morning, how are you? Can you do a favor for me, and stand here while I run down to the main office and get my walkie-talkie? Ms. Carrington is supposed to let me know when the mayor, superintendent, and president of the school board are on their way to the building. Actually, never mind, I'll walk down there myself in a few minutes."

"Oh, so we have visitors this morning?" Peyton asked in a sarcastic tone, giving Jackson a half-smile, and wink.

"Yeah and you've been here long enough so you know how it goes. The dog and pony show for the cameras on the first day of school. They want to come around here and make it seem like they doing all they can do for these poor, Black kids. In what world, is all I say to that? I'm pretty sure I won't see this bunch again all year."

Jackson shrugged his shoulders and continued. "I'll play their game, as long as they don't mess with my budget or pick on me about talking to the media and making comments about how poorly they're doing their goddamn jobs."

"Now, Mr. Jackson, don't you go getting yourself all worked up and into trouble. It's only the first day and it's a long way to June." Peyton laughed as she began her walk down the hallway. "I'll see you later after your dog and pony show."

"Always the funny one, Ms. Stanfield, always the funny one," Jackson chimed, as he watched her walk away. According to Gina, who once upon a time had a crush on Principal Jackson, he was a big, harmless flirt. His and Peyton's relationship was genuinely friendly. They met several years prior when she operated an afterschool program in the building next to his building. At the time, she sensed he might have a romantic interest, but nothing ever matriculated and she left and returned to her primary school and didn't see him again until her assignment as one of the social workers in his building. She emailed him about it, but never received a return response. He was truly surprised that first day of school three years ago when she showed up looking for her office location.

There were plenty rumors of Jackson carrying on school romances, but Peyton had no firsthand knowledge of any so-called trysts, which was the norm in Charm Town schools where there was a handsome, male leader. Peyton, over the years, had direct knowledge of at least three situations when teachers became romantically involved with the principal, most notably during her time at Indian Hill. There were a fair number of attractive teachers in the building and the separated principal, Mr. Goings, was having a time sampling all the interest in him. She found Mr. Goings attractive, but was too busy trying to garner the attention of one Trinidadian named Mark to consider him. She couldn't help but smile when she thought of their mutual attraction. The full romance never blossomed, but a friendship did. Infrequent phone calls and periodic meetups for drinks and crabs maintained the relationship.

A number of female teachers in the building had strong attractions for Jackson. The latest rumor, started by the music teacher last year, was that he was dating the language arts teacher, Ms. Jordan. No one really liked her and Peyton couldn't understand the attraction, but to each his own. He was young, single and enjoyed the attention of women. He also enjoyed a good happy hour from time to time, his method of relaxing after a challenging week at the school.

Jackson's upbeat and fair attitude, professional treatment of his staff and willingness to help wherever needed was admirable. He was one of a few district principals who understood he needed the teachers and support staff in his building and that it was suicide for him, in the role of principal, to alienate, harass, and intimidate his building staff. The staff could make or break a principal and ruin reputations with their silent strong work ethic or with silent resistance. Peyton heard stories about principals who intentionally cultivated an environment of distrust and manipulation, often preying on the non-tenured and timid staff. She remembered Principal Tot Golding blocking the transfer of a single-parent teacher, conducting sneaky classroom observations and completing unfair performance evaluations. She learned in her early years, that the number of cars present in the parking lot hours after the school bell rung for dismissal was a strong indicator of the effectiveness and likeability of a principal.

Peyton walked down the hallway, passed excited students at their lockers greeting each other and talking about summer's antics, toward her office. She needed to sign in at the main office, but decided she would wait until later in the morning. Luckily, the school secretary, Ms. Carrington, and Principal Jackson weren't one of those sign-in book gangsters who got pleasure out of grabbing the book out of staff's hands not a second after the late time. The main office and guidance office, on the first day, were always flooded with parents and students wanting to register, get a class schedule, or request a transfer. She was sure Ms. Carrington had her hands full and needed no more distractions.

"Peyton, Peyton! Stop, wait a minute."

She heard her name loudly called by an anxious, familiar voice. She stopped, turned, and saw Gina walking very quickly toward her, ignoring all the kids in the hallway who stared at her.

"Hey lady, welcome to the first day of school. What's up? You ready to leave out the building already?" Peyton jokingly said, as Gina grew near.

Gina spoke before she reached her. "Quick, come to my office, I need to talk with you."

Peyton sensed her urgency, but remained calm. "Right now? I was on my way to my office to see what's been lifted by the summer crew and then I have to get to the alternative ed office and get my caseload. I might have an SAP meeting as soon as tomorrow and I want to get myself prepared. I'll be back down in a few minutes."

"Blah, blah, blah. I need you to come with me now! You're always shouting something off about those SAP meetings. That can wait, this won't. Trust me you'll be glad I came and found you." Gina grabbed Peyton by the arm and escorted her to her office. They looked like two teenage girls running off to giggle about something childish.

Both entered Gina's naturally lit office. She had a keen eye for décor, having obtained a certificate in interior design in college. Plants, pictures, books applicable for the students and plenty of posters that reminded the students of expectations to achieve and succeed adorned her office. One of the many things Peyton admired about Gina was her commitment to her students, particularly those who came from hard family circumstances. When it came to kids, especially kids who endured the raw deal of life, her heart was full of pure genuineness.

Peyton dropped her purse and bag, and sank down into one of her leather chairs. "Okay, so what the hell is up? You got me a *little* scared."

Gina brandished her girlish, gossipy look. "Girl, guess who is coming to the building this morning? I happened to be in the main office when Ms. Carrington got the call."

"Who? The president?" Peyton asked in a sarcastic tone. "Actually, Jackson already told me that the mayor, superintendent, and president of the school board are coming."

"Well, the Mayor's office just called and cancelled saying he has an urgent matter to attend to. But…Mr. Hamilton Banks is coming. Remember him? Of course, you remember, as you said it, his fine ass. He's coming with his wife, Sandra Banks, who just happens to be the president of the Charm Town school board. Her office told Ms. Carrington that he was accompanying her as she visits schools this morning because he's planning to adopt a school for the year and this year it's Montebello. Apparently, he's big into that philanthropy shit and picks a school each year that he gives money to and something about mentoring some kids."

"Are you serious?" Peyton sat upright in the chair, suddenly very interested in what Gina said.

"Yep, they should be here within the hour. Now, what do you think about that, missy? Still want to rush up to your office and that damn alternative ed room?" Gina sat back in her chair with her arms crossed in front of her, obviously proud of herself for delivering this unexpected news.

"I don't know just yet. What should I think? He doesn't know I work here." Peyton rose, grabbed her cosmetic bag out her purse, and checked her hair and makeup in Gina's mirror on the wall. "He might not even remember me."

"*Shit*, yes he will." Gina smirked, as she now sat upright in her chair. "I knew you would want to know this and the fact that he *is married* and not just to any random woman."

"Wow, I know. He didn't strike me as a married person. Although he did have on a band, his energy just didn't give off that of someone who is married, or maybe I just didn't care. We social workers call that denial." Peyton remained in the mirror, smoothed out her blush, and applied more mascara and lip-gloss.

"So, what are you *going to* do?" Gina gave Peyton the side-eye.

"What do you mean what am I going to do? I'm *going to* go about doing my job of helping these kids and if I should happen to run into Mr. Banks, then I will not be rude and not speak." Peyton playfully spoke in an English style proper tone.

"I'm sure you will." Gina looked at Peyton with a raised brow and pursed lips.

"You can't fool me chick. You know you're happy about this. You couldn't stop talking about his ass once you came out that restaurant and now a mere few days later, he is showing up at your place of employment. I'd say you are having a darn good week."

"I'm just glad I decided to wear this skirt and sandals. Do you think I look sexy?" Peyton turned from side to side, providing Gina with a full view of her outfit.

"Girl, bye. You know you look good." She smiled at her friend.

"Okay, well I really got to go. I can't spend a bunch of time in here with you, wondering if this man is going to actually show up. I got kids to see but thanks for the heads up." Peyton grabbed her bags and headed to the door. She stopped and turned back to Gina. "So, Mr. Hamilton Banks is about to be on my territory. Hmmm, interesting, *very* interesting. I'll see you later, Gina." She grinned, walked out and up a flight of stairs to her office.

Chapter Five

As expected, students surrounded Peyton's office, wanting something on the first day of school. It was normal for Charm Town students to run to the room of their favorite person to report on summer activities.

"Ms. Stanfield, hello!" Justice Dawkins ran to Peyton, arms stretched out, ready to give a hug. "I missed you this summer."

Peyton saw Justice headed her way, but her focus was on clearing the area of students near her office.

"Let's get to class, ladies and gentleman," she called out to the small groups of students who lingered in the hallway after the bell rung. She hoped the hall monitors would be conducting a hall sweep soon. The first day of school was always the best time to enforce school law. It created a more organized year and students understood, from day one, nonsense wasn't tolerated. Once her voice rang out, most of the students moved to where they needed to report. A few continued to linger and she gave them another verbal nudge as she stood with her hands on her waist. "Let's go, *let's go*. It's the first day, folks, and I need you to get moving to where you are supposed to be. There will be plenty time for chitchat at lunch or afterschool. You can all catch up and hug each other then. Right now, it's time to get to class." The remaining students eyed her as if they wanted to respond but moved along. She never got much resistance from the kids. They liked her and her reputation was positive with them.

"Hey, Justice, how are you?" She embraced her with one arm while carrying her purse and briefcase in the other. "Let me open my door and we can talk for a bit. Where is your first period class?"

"Oh, I have Ms. Rich for first period. I already saw her and told her I wanted to come and see you. She said it was okay." Justice smiled apprehensively; clearly, she wanted to share something. Biracial, a mixture of African American and Korean descent, she was dressed in full uniform with her hair freshly colored with a hint of blond streaks. Peyton suddenly realized Justice never talked about her Korean family and she made a mental note to ask her about them.

"Okay, cool." Peyton's office and desk were just as she left them in June, except with a lot of dust from the summer. She set her things down and immediately grabbed her Pledge wipes from her desk drawer and wiped down her furniture. Self-help books and treatment books she accumulated over the years at conferences and through professional sites such as The National Association of Social Workers or the American Psychological Association filled her office. There were always scores of organizations ready to sell books and journals on helping others. The system wasn't able to pay for those materials or pay to send clinicians to attend conferences sponsored by those organizations. There never seemed to be enough money for those sorts of things, noticeably in schools with populations of primarily poor, minority kids.

Justice Dawkins was a seventeen-year-old, honor roll, senior at Montebello, who was stunningly beautiful and often compared to a young Kimora. Popular, smart, and artistically talented, she endured tragedy and pain in her young life. She lived with her grandmother and grandfather who raised her when her father killed her mother in a murder-suicide when she was two years old.

Her father was away in his home country of Korea and returned to Charm Town. Apparently, her parents fought and, one day, her father came to the house she lived in, kicked in the door, and barricaded him and her mother in the house. He strangled her, set the home on fire, and then shot himself in the head. By the time the fire fighters and paramedics arrived, the house was fully ablaze and they were unable to save them. Luckily, Justice was in daycare. Her grandparents insisted her mother enroll her in the Blossoming Seeds program. As a low-income family, Justice's mother secured full-time registration, tuition, and transportation for a small monthly fee. It allowed her mother a chance to look for better employment and attend school and allowed Justice the opportunity to socialize with other children her age. One year later, the unthinkable happened again to her family. Neighborhood drug dealers shot her mother's sister, her only sibling, and her entire family to death as they walked home from Druid Park because the family repeatedly complained to police about the rampant drug sales on their residential street. It was a story that caught the attention of the entire town and beyond. The Mayor and other town officials attended the funerals and there was a street and park in the town named in their honor.

Justice was the remaining offspring of the Dawkins family. Well known throughout the town because of her family's misfortunes, she was the subject of numerous news stories. A number of community activists and do-gooders contributed money toward the expenses of raising her. Now, at seventeen, with depleted funds, most of the do-gooders were gone.

"So, what's up?" Peyton asked Justice. "You look like you have something on your mind."

Tears started to flow and Justice wasted no time blurting out her troubles.

"I'm pregnant. Three months pregnant and now, my boyfriend isn't talking to me. He wants me to get an abortion. Ms. Stanfield, I don't know what to do. I kept telling him I thought I might be pregnant when I didn't get my menstrual the last two months. Finally, he went to the Save-A-Lot and got a pregnancy test and it was positive." Justice sobbed, as she slumped down in the chair. "I'm supposed to go to college, but I want to keep my baby. I don't think I can do it Ms. Stanfield, but I'm also scared that I won't be able to give my baby what it needs. You know what it's been like for me."

Peyton hid her surprise and disappointment, walked around her desk to comfort Justice, and handed her a tissue from the box on her desk. Tissues were an essential supply for her office and the classrooms of all the teachers. There were many students in the building who dealt with unimaginable pain inflicted mostly by the adults in their lives—physical and sexual abuse, substance abuse, domestic violence, mental health challenges and abandonment. When they made it to her office and began sharing their stories, the tears usually weren't far behind. She developed a reputation of one who listened to students and sympathized with their individual circumstances, even if she couldn't offer a solution or remove the pain. In her office, she ensured her students didn't feel obscure.

"Try and calm yourself, Justice. Would you like to talk about it more?" She started to wonder what this girl was going to do because she essentially had no family support. Her grandparents were nice, but elderly, tired and grief-stricken. They barely kept up with her life, not able to attend her school theatre productions or volleyball games. They missed teacher conferences and last year's College Night Seminar for rising seniors and their parents. Due to the family circumstances, Peyton agreed to conduct home visits with her grandparents to bring school information to them. On many occasions, they expressed their desire for Justice to attend college. She would be the first in her family to graduate high school and further her studies. Her grandparents couldn't see any other way for her to make it out of her current situation. They came from the generation of Black people in Charm Town who participated in civil rights rallies and sit-ins for the right to vote and get an equal education. They knew and understood firsthand the struggles and sacrifices of those before Justice and they wanted to see her benefit.

"Have you told your grandparents?"

"Yes." Justice was still sobbing.

"Okay, so what did they say?"

"My grandma said I will have to leave and find someplace else to stay if I have a baby. She said she and papa can't afford any formula or diapers." Peyton, surprised by their reaction, immediately became angry. Yes, they were elderly, tired and grief-stricken, but she saw too many parents and caregivers throw young girls out into the streets because they were pregnant. This was the time when they needed support and stability the most. She'd never heard of a situation where parents threw out their sons because they got a girl pregnant.

"It's okay, honey." Peyton put her arm around Justice to try to console her. "I'm here ready to talk about all of this when you are ready. Have you been to the doctor, do you know how far along you are?"

"No, I go to the doctor's next week. My grandma said she doesn't have time to take me plus I don't think I could get an appointment until next week."

"Okay, do you know where your doctor is located?"

"At John Memorial Hospital, but I don't want to stay there. I heard they be snatching girls' babies over there right when they born and giving them to child services and putting them in foster care. I don't want my baby to go to foster care, Ms. Stanfield."

Peyton continued to keep her arm around Justice. "Let's not get all worked up about all that right now. What's important now is that you start seeing a doctor on a regular basis and start receiving prenatal care. I know you want to make sure your baby is healthy, right?"

"Oh yeah. Ain't nothing going to happen to my baby and I am not giving my baby to no child services. I'm telling you right now, Ms. Stanfield, I'm not doing it and they better not try and make me do it." Peyton saw the seriousness in Justice's eyes.

"I really don't think you will need to worry about that."

She saw that Justice became increasingly emotional and she decided to shift the conversation. "Tell me about your schedule this year. Do you like it?"

Justice didn't have time to answer because the bell rang, and it was time for her to move to her next class. She wiped her face and motioned to Peyton that she wanted to stand up. "Can we talk later, Ms. Stanfield? I gotta go."

"Sure, Justice. I should be here for at least an hour afterschool if you want to stop back here. If not, I'll be here bright and early tomorrow morning."

"Okay, I'll do that. You got some candy or snacks? I didn't get to eat breakfast before I left out this morning."

"No, sorry, not today. It's the first day of school and I haven't stocked up yet." Peyton let out a giggle. "Plus, you are now eating for two and you must remember to eat healthy and often and drink lots of water. That little baby growing inside of you needs good nutrients, but we'll talk about all that another time."

"Okay, I hear you. I'm out. Thanks, Ms. Stanfield. Hey, I'm glad you're back. I was worried you might have moved to another school over the summer. The last social worker I had in my other school was moved over the summer and we never even got to say goodbye. I heard she was made to move or lose her job. I thought that was so unfair." Justice dried her eyes with the tissue, gave Peyton a half smile, and left out of the office.

❧

Still thinking about Justice five minutes later, Peyton unpacked her bag, stood and looked around her office.

What is this year going to be like? How many of my kids will get into trouble, fail some classes, get suspended, get arrested, get caught up in that sex trafficking stuff that is rampant here, get pregnant, get hospitalized for trying to kill themselves or having depression, get an STD, or get killed? How many parents will not come up to this school to check on their child, return my or the teacher's phone calls, attend the PTA meetings, come to the back-to-school-night event, attend report card conferences, volunteer, conduct random, surprise visits to their child's classroom or help to raise money for needed school supplies, equipment and materials?

She also knew there was plenty good with her students.

Most of these students in the building and across this town attend school every day, pay attention in class and work hard to get good grades. Most of the students are well behaved and eager to learn. Most of the students are gifted in some way academically, athletically, or artistically. Most of the students want to do better and many strive to graduate high school and attend college because they are first generation kids. Most of these students know what it means to want more for themselves, their families, their schools, their communities, and their towns. They just need the district and state officials to take them more seriously and recognize there are some really great kids in the town and to stop making bullshit excuses as to why their schools look the worst in the state.

The loud speaker interrupted her thoughts. It was Principal Jackson.

"Pardon this interruption, but will all of the mental health practitioners in the building report to the main office immediately?" That was all he said and the loudspeaker went dead.

Peyton knew his announcement was about the visitors and the visit Gina was all too happy to tell her about. She grabbed her purse, searched again for her cosmetic bag, hoping she hadn't left it in Gina's office. She reminded herself to switch to smaller purses because those big designer bags she carried around always seemed to hide the stuff she needed the most, like her makeup case. She finally found it and pulled out her Chanel lip-gloss and MAC blusher. She wanted to look fresh for him.

Silly girl, what are you doing? This man is married and you are way too excited to see him.

As she applied her gloss and blusher, she couldn't help but giggle a little. She felt like a sixteen-year-old about to meet her teenage crush for the first time. She finished applying her look, packed up her cosmetics, and placed her purse in her bottom desk drawer. She then headed out the door down to the main office. It was time to go see her man.

❧

Nearing the office, she saw him. There he stood, tall and delicious wearing an expensive-looking tailored, dark, navy suit with a crisp white shirt open at the neck with no tie. The other day was no stroke of luck. He was still gorgeous.

Damn it, why does he have to be so fine?

She couldn't believe how her heart raced as she walked toward the group. She and the other mental health providers in the building quickly reported to the main office. Peyton smoothed out her skirt as she continued toward them. As she approached, he looked up, recognized her, and flashed the widest, most beautiful grin she ever saw. She realized she smiled back. She also realized he wore that silver band on his ring finger.

"Ms. Stanfield, please come," Principal Jackson waved for her to enter in the front area of the main office. Peyton walked into the office and joined Jackson, her colleagues, and the distinguished guests.

"Everyone, please allow me to introduce our lead school social worker, Ms. Peyton Stanfield. She has been with us now for several years and has developed an excellent relationship with our students, especially those students who have had some rough starts in life."

"Hello, everyone," Peyton said, as she established eye contact, careful not to look at him any longer than the others. She instantly felt warm, her hands sweated, and her face looked flush.

Just stand here and smile, don't move, she repeated to herself.

Principal Jackson continued. "Let me introduce our guests and share with you a wonderful opportunity that has been brought to our school and students this year." He pointed to each of the guests. "This is Superintendent Dianna Evans, President of the School Board, Sandra Banks and her husband, businessman Hamilton Banks. Mr. Banks has generously adopted our school this year. He plans to help us with funding and mentor some of our challenging students. In addition, the superintendent has committed extra funds to us to help with our issue of dropout students." Principal Jackson stood and smiled, as he displayed his fake enthusiasm. Mentally, Peyton rolled her eyes.

Sure, they want to help out, by doing what? Jackson was right. They always say they want to help and then we never hear anything more....until the next year or next photo op.

Principal Jackson turned to Peyton. "Ms. Stanfield, I would like to assign you as the school contact for Mr. Banks to work with this year. As our lead social worker, you are most aware of the students and families at our school who are in need. I also think you are best suited to help Mr. Banks figure out how he could assist us."

Suddenly, Hamilton stepped forward from the other two. His presence commanded everyone's attention.

"Mr. Jackson, Charm Town, and its schools have been a passion of mine for some time now. I went to school here in Charm Town. It was a private school, but I had friends who went to the neighborhood schools and I remember what it was like for them. I'm excited about helping you and your staff to make the lives of some of your kids better. That's what I'm about. I'm part of a family legacy of giving back and I am honored."

Peyton stood motionless and stared directly at him. She noticed his wife also stared at him.

If he keeps saying all the right things, I just might lose it right here and really embarrass myself. Come on, just get yourself together. You are not in high school or college. This is your job. You can flirt with him later.

"Thank you, Mr. Banks." Principal Jackson looked proud and grateful. "I'm sure you and Ms. Stanfield will be able to work out some wonderful things for our kids this year. Peyton, would you please take Mr. Banks to your office for a bit and begin to map out what he would like to contribute for this year?"

She hoped the look on her face in no way matched her feelings.

Please, don't make me go off somewhere alone with this man, passed through her mind.

He'll surely see right through me and feel my intense attraction.

"Sure, Principal Jackson, I'm happy to," she said as she masked her excitement and nervousness.

Peyton smiled at the group and turned to Hamilton.

"Mr. Banks, my office is on the second floor, so I hope you don't mind taking the steps."

He removed his suit jacket and draped it across his left arm. "Not at all, please lead the way. Sandra, I will meet you down here in…how long will you all be meeting?"

"Give us about forty-five minutes and we should be all wrapped up," Sandra Banks said in a very formal, smart voice. Peyton walked toward the door.

She looks like someone nobody would want to play with or expect to be the winner in a catfight with her.

"Okay, we'll be back in forty-five minutes, if not sooner." She felt his presence as he walked closely behind.

Remain calm, just remain calm.

You cannot appear as if you are some dumb social worker. Get yourself together and find out what he wants. He puts his pants on one leg at a time like you, so just be yourself.

"Good to see you again, Ms. Stanfield." Hamilton spoke first, as he walked alongside her.

He is walking a little too close, but, damn, he smells good.

"I'm surprised you remember my name." She thought of nothing else to say. She felt stupid, but his amazingly good looks captured her focus. She hoped he hadn't felt her sexual energy.

Lord Jesus can you please help me? How will I ever make it through an entire school year with him? Somebody is in trouble and it's probably my ass.

"Now, why wouldn't I remember your name, Ms. Stanfield? You introduced yourself to me just the other day. I hope you enjoyed the bread pudding." He had a naughty grin on his face and she was sure he flirted with her.

"It was delicious, Mr. Banks. You definitely have a winner there."

"Oh, please call me Hamilton, and may I call you Peyton? If we are going to be working together this year, I suppose we should be on first name basis, right?" His naughty grin transitioned to a smirk.

Damn it, he knows I have the hots for him, he knows it, I just know he knows it.

"Okay, Hamilton, first name basis it is."

As they continued to walk, one of her students approached them. "Hey, Ms. Stanfield, I'm gonna come and see you either before school is out or tomorrow," Isaiah Young blurted out.

Peyton and Hamilton stopped. "Okay, Isaiah, that's fine. You're doing well?"

"Yeah, I'm doing good, just gotta hurry and get to Mr. Barnes' class. He doesn't play that late stuff and might try to mess around and give me a detention on the first day of school. Who does that?"

"Just get yourself there, Isaiah, and I'll see you either later or tomorrow." Peyton was happy for the small distraction, she was so nervous she felt sweat balls forming in her armpits, *again.*

"Okay, Ms. Stanfield. I'll see you later. It was a little crazy around the way this summer but I'll come and tell you all about it." Isaiah walked hurriedly down the hallway toward his classroom.

Peyton returned her focus to Hamilton. "That's one of my students who has had a hard time, but has managed to do well in school. I just hope he can stay out of trouble this year because he has a lot of negativity around him. It's in his family, on his block, with some of his friends, everywhere. However, he's a really smart and good kid. I'm working with him now on letting go of some old anger and thinking about college."

"Is he now?" Hamilton sounded interested. "Maybe he can be one of my mentees, if you think that would be a good idea, Ms. Stanfield."

There he goes, being flirty again. There is no stopping this man. He knows exactly what he is doing with those eyes and that body. Who is his trainer?

They finally arrived to Peyton's office. As she turned the key in the door lock, she felt the warmth of his body behind her, as she inhaled the fantastic smell of his cologne. It mixed perfectly with his body chemistry. She opened the door and welcomed Hamilton Banks into her space. She closed the door behind them and instantly wondered if that was a mistake.

He might try something and I might not be able to resist.

"Please have a seat, Hamilton," she said, as she noticed him looking interestingly around her office—first at the books on her shelves and then at the posters on her walls. He lastly viewed the pictures she had on her desk of her parents, siblings, and friends on trips they took over the years.

Hmm, he clearly seems intrigued.

"So, Peyton, what would you like to do with me this year?" He sat down, and looked directly into her eyes.

He really shouldn't do that.

She suspected he knew she was extremely attracted to him.

Are you seriously going to ask me that question? What would I like to do with you? How about fuck your brains out, for starters. See just what you are working with down there in those pants.

"I'm not sure, Mr. Banks, excuse me, I mean, Hamilton. Why don't you tell me a little bit about what your interests are and what you think you might be able to contribute to our student population." She tried to sound professional.

Suddenly, he leaned forward, rested his arms on her desk, and stared into her eyes.

"I thought I might not ever see you again. I've been thinking about you since you left the café and I come in here today, and here you are. Can't be anything but fate, Ms. Stanfield. What do you think?"

"Me? What do I think? Well, first I thought you were going to call me Peyton." She was unsure of anything more to say.

Get yourself together and talk with this man as if you have good sense.

"I'm sorry…Peyton."

She relaxed a bit and smiled.

"Well it certainly was a nice surprise to see you here this morning. I didn't think I would see you again so soon and certainly not today."

"Listen, I know we need to come up with a plan for the year and don't get me wrong, that's what I want to do. I'm genuinely interested and serious about helping out these kids. I'm always telling Sandra how, yes, Charm Town has done some good things for its students, but a whole lot of those students were robbed of a good, decent education and have, basically, been left behind. They are the kids I want to help. Those kids who were born and bred in the hood and have never been more than two miles outside the hood. It's a shame that most of them haven't even been to a museum downtown or visited the other side of this town. Heck, half of them don't even know the other side exists. I'm sorry but I could go on and on."

"Its okay, Hamilton, I can hear the sincerity and passion in your voice. It's—"

He cut her off. "Can we do this some other time, talk about all this? Right now, I want to spend the rest of the time I am here in this office learning about you. I'm attracted to you, Ms. Stanfield, and I would like to invite you to join me for lunch this Saturday at The Lucky Café. Would you be interested and able to do that?"

He was serious.

Yes, hell yes, is what she wanted to say, *but he's married, he's married* was imprinted on her brain.

"Hamilton....I don't want to come off as rude, but you are married and I have met your wife, although briefly and I don't make it a habit to see married men." She paused briefly. "I guess I'm feeling a bit uncomfortable with all this." She stared at him, the sweat still forming under her blouse.

"I understand, Ms. Stanfield, and I certainly don't wish for you to feel uncomfortable. You don't know this about me, and honest to God I am not ignoring what I think you are trying to tell me, but I'm a man that likes getting what he wants and right now, I want to have lunch with you, this Saturday at two o'clock in my restaurant. I will ask you again. Do you think you can make it?"

Well, what could lunch hurt? She was interested in his thoughts on helping the students. She could get some food and talk about the work. She tried hard to convince herself that this was okay, that it would be all-good.

She didn't need long to decide.

You better say something because he's going to keep staring at you smiling at him.

"Okay, Hamilton, I accept your invitation. Saturday at two it is."

"Wonderful. I look forward to it." Peyton barely heard Hamilton's response because Principal Jackson's voice came over the loudspeaker.

"Excuse this interruption, but will Mr. Hamilton Banks please report to the main office. Mr. Hamilton Banks, please report to the main office. Thank you." Two seconds later, Peyton's phone rang. She recognized the extension as that of Jackson.

"Hello, Peyton Stanfield speaking." She watched Hamilton watch her as she answered the call.

I just cannot believe this man, on this day, is here in my office and asking me out. Wait 'til I tell Gina about this.

"Ms. Stanfield is Mr. Banks still with you in your office?"

"Yes, he is here." Hamilton continued to stare at her.

Hasn't anyone ever told him it is rude to stare? She figured not. A man of Hamilton's stature probably didn't have many people telling him much, including his wife. Peyton wondered what was up with that situation.

"Okay, great. Will you please escort him back to the main office? Mrs. Banks has been called back to the administration offices and her driver is waiting outside."

"Sure, Principal Jackson, no problem. We are on our way down." She was thankful for the interruption because she was sure Hamilton was going to start in on asking question after question. She hung up the phone.

"Apparently, your wife has to get back to the district and she is waiting for you in the main office. We have to leave now, but if you want, we can arrange another time to meet about this on Saturday."

"That would be great, Ms. Stanfield, and do you have to mention my wife? I'm quite aware I am married." Hamilton rose up from the chair. "But before we are back around others, I want to tell you there was something about you that attracted me to you immediately. There's no denying the fact you are a beautiful and clearly a confident woman, but that's not it. I have no idea what it is about you yet, but I do know I am looking forward to this Saturday and talking with you. Thank you for accepting my invitation."

He is a polite man.

She ignored his question about his wife.

"It's no problem, Hamilton, and thanks for the invitation. I look forward to talking school business with you. Now we better get going."

He reached out and grabbed her arm to stop her, as she walked by him toward the door. Once again, he looked into her eyes.

"I'm really happy I ran into you here. I had no idea when or where I would see you again and I've been thinking about you. I look forward to preparing a nice lunch for you." His grin and smile were irresistible. He released her arm and grabbed her hand, kissing the back.

She felt the knot in her stomach, but managed to smile as their eyes locked for a few seconds.

Don't you dare kiss him, and if he tries to kiss me, I'll turn my head.

They both walked out the door, down the hallway and stairwell in silence toward the main office and his wife.

Chapter Six

Back-to-school night was the time when parents came to the school at the beginning of the year to meet with their child's teachers and the school staff. The principal usually spoke in the beginning, sharing the vision for the school and spent a majority of the time explaining to the parents why the school was the best place for their child and how they had big plans to prepare the students for graduation, college, and careers. Most of the teachers used the opportunity to explain their teaching styles, class curriculum, grading policy, assignments, and individual class rules. They told the parents of their hopes for their child and their expectations of them in their classroom. They also discussed behavior and some of the teachers of the senior students talked about college choice, and what students needed to do to begin the application, and financial aid process. The parents got an opportunity to see their child's classroom, sit in their seats at their desks, and visualize a typical day in the classroom.

Peyton didn't always attend the event, but this time she decided to go. She spoke with several of the other teachers in the teacher's lounge earlier that day and they all talked about the speech Principal Jackson planned to deliver to parents.

One particular teacher, Carmen Murphy, who taught AP biology, looked forward to his comments. She was the first to speak in the lounge.

"So Peyton, are you coming tonight? I can't *wait* to hear what Jackson is going to say, especially after that article in the paper from the other day. *The Charm Town Times* really hooked him up."

"Yeah, it sure does read that way. I wasn't planning to come, but I changed my mind. I'm kinda interested in what Jackson is going to say myself. You know, many times, it ends up being not a good use of my time. Almost none of my kids' parents come to talk with me or any of the other clinicians, although they should."

"You're right, but you never know, this might be the year *all* your parents come and want to talk to you about how they can rid their kid of the effects of their shit."

Carmen rolled her eyes. "Plus, a bunch of us are thinking about going out afterward to get some drinks. I know there is supposed to be dinner here, but drinks are always good. I'm not bold like some of the folks around here, who shall remain nameless, who think its okay to carry a little something more than water, tea or coffee in their cup."

Suddenly, all the attention was on Carmen who loved attention.

"What? Y'all want to act as if you don't know what I'm talking about? You know as well as I that Hennessey and Absolut are a staple in some of the cups around here."

Peyton and some of the others nodded, but remained silent.

Carmen was the teacher who loved to party and have fun. She was twenty-five years old with no cares in the world. A part-time bartender at The Brewer's Art, a hip bar in Charm Town, she sampled almost as much alcohol as she served. Peyton enjoyed her Monday morning tales of her weekend, one-night hookups. She came to Montebello two years ago as part of the Youth Teachers program. She was very knowledgeable in her subject content, but struggled with classroom management. The students were sometimes disrespectful toward her and didn't always listen when she tried to establish order in her classroom. Luckily, her classroom was next to Mr. Rich, a veteran math teacher. He got her class to settle down and focus on her lesson.

"Where are you going?" Peyton tried to sound interested, but her mind wandered to thoughts of Hamilton.

"Maybe down to Tavern on the Square. I was going to suggest Brewer's, but they might try and get me to work and tonight I just want to relax and have someone wait on me for a change."

"I hear you. I can imagine it might be a little awkward sitting on the other side of the bar. Especially that bar." Peyton laughed.

"Yeah, it is and tonight I just don't feel like dealing with those people. So are you going to hang out with us afterward?"

"Ah, maybe. I'll think about it."

Recently, a local news station featured Principal Jackson in a segment about up-and-coming educators in the Charm Town district. Peyton remembered the day the reporter and news cameras showed up at the building and interviewed him. For two hours, they walked the hallways, filmed students in the classroom, and students who interacted with Jackson. It was a proud moment for Jackson and Peyton and the staff were happy for him. She felt he definitely deserved the recognition because the district had not done so. They actually spent a lot of time attempting to discredit him by offering minimal support and flooding the school with more students and no increase in funding. That seemed to be how things were done with administrators who actually made a difference with the students and weren't afraid to challenge the Charm Town central office when student needs were the issue.

Peyton arrived back at the school thirty minutes before the start of the program. Unlike some of her colleagues, she went home to shower and change into clothing that was more comfortable. She headed to the library to meet her colleagues and check out the dinner spread. That was the customary plan for back-to-school night. The principal found money from somewhere in the budget, usually from a business partner, to buy food for the staff. It was a nice gesture and the staff appreciated it. The dinner consisted of platters of different sandwiches with several selections of salad from Eddie's Market, which was a popular selection of the school for staff meals. Peyton walked in to find Ms. Edna, the lead school custodian and undercover comedian, setting up tables. She was a petite woman with the skin of someone who may have had a prior issue with a drug or two. She sported short silver-colored hair perfectly curled and round glasses that fit perfectly on her round face. The uniform she wore to work looked as if it was fresh out the dry cleaners, neat and starched. A nice woman, she proudly exhibited a smart mouth and no-nonsense attitude. She, too, had the respect of the students who called her Grandma.

"Hey there Ms. Edna, what's going on? You need some help?"

"Really, Ms. Stanfield? You *really* want to help me? If so, you are the first. Everybody else has come in here or walked past here, seen me setting up these tables and chairs by myself and nobody decided to ask if I needed a damn thing. They too busy helping themselves to one another. Y'all think I don't know about a certain music teacher and a certain gym teacher getting it on in the Phys Ed office?"

Uh oh, here she goes. How did she find out about that? I just found out myself. This woman knows everything that goes on around here as most custodians do.

Peyton pretended to look shocked.

"Ms. Edna, what on earth are you talking about?"

Ms. Edna smirked at Peyton.

"You know what the hell I'm talking about. I'm talking about these teachers around here acting like they can't find nobody else to date but themselves and it don't even matter if they married. Is marriage respected by anyone anymore? I mean, damn, when I was coming along, you kept your hands off somebody's husband. There may have been some who slipped up, but that was few and far between. Nowadays, it's just whatever. You see somebody and want him or her; you just go after him or her. There's no respect among you young folk no more. I don't understand it 'cause if somebody went after my husband, I'd take a bat to their head."

Oh no, Ms. Edna has gotten started. Is she going to give me her marriage-is-sacred-and-special-and-spiritual talk? Peyton felt uncomfortable and aware of the sweat formed on her forehead, as she listened to Ms. Edna like an obedient child.

"Every school I've worked in, from the principal on down to us, yes, us the custodians, there has been either rumor or fact of some hanky-panky. There is more sex among the adults around these schools than folk would want to believe. You remember several years ago that story that was in the news about the teacher who was accidentally burned in the science lab? That happened at my old school and that story was a big ass lie. What really happened was the tech teacher, a real ladies man, was having something going on with one of the art teachers and they got into some kind of argument and she ended up getting burned. They weren't in the science lab; they were in the Culinary Arts classroom. Fucking around on the tables where them kids learning to be chefs and be putting their food. His wife was calling the principal, asking why he had a home wrecker as a teacher in his building and did he know all this was going on in the building and she should sue. Now sue for what, I don't know. Men and women cheating have been going on for centuries and will continue to go for centuries more. It was a mess."

Peyton knew she was stuck with this lecture for a bit longer.

"Isn't that something? Don't ask me how the burn actually happened."

Ms. Edna shook her head.

"It's all crazy to me because they so sloppy with their shit and almost always the kids find out about it and then there is that mess of having immature ass kids knowing grown folks business. See, when I was coming along in school, we never knew about no teachers having sex at all, let alone with each other. I don't know, I guess people's standards have changed over the years. It's probably all this crazy shit we seeing on cable television and them reality shows."

As Ms. Edna talked, Peyton remembered her own turn with an office romance, which wasn't really an office romance. She liked one of the teachers in her first school. A week before school ended, at the advice of another friend at the time, who assured her this teacher was single, she began sending him anonymous gifts each day for one week with the last gift revealing her identity. In the end, she was embarrassed because it turned out this teacher was involved with someone. Peyton was grateful for two things: he was sweet when he informed her of his status, although he made a comment about her being careful about where she got her information, and to her knowledge, he never told anyone. The private rejection between them was shameful enough.

Peyton knew Ms. Edna could go on and on, so she interjected. "I'm sorry about that, Ms. Edna. What can I say? Some folks have home training, values, and morals and some don't."

"You got that shit right." Ms. Edna was never short for words and many of them were profane. She was what Peyton considered real-never faked her thoughts and actions for anyone. She worked for Charm Town for more than twenty-five years and had her fair share of stories about the schools that Peyton loved to hear. She also was a very smart woman, although she never achieved her high school diploma. Peyton always believed some of the staff talked down to her or turned their noses up at her because she was the custodian, never bothering to speak as they passed her in the halls. The funny thing was Ms. Edna was aware of them and would say, "these uppity-ass bitches get on my damn nerves, walking around here like they so much better than everybody else."

Peyton laughed and told Ms. Edna not to worry about them and she always had a response. "I'm not worried about a damn thing because if any one of these ho's try to fuck with me, I'm going to tell all the shit and not just to the folks downtown. They don't know that I know what really goes on around here and in some of the other schools I've worked, people think that the custodians are stupid and don't know what's going on. Chile, I've seen more sex, drugs, and missing cash in my years than anyone would ever believe. And, some of the stuff I've seen lying around in principal's offices would shock the hell out you, too. Let's just say that if I were a drinker, I wouldn't need to visit a liquor store. There is more top shelf liquor in principal's offices than the damn liquor stores themselves. And it wouldn't be a lie if I told you I've found some weed once or twice, too."

Peyton developed an instant rapport with Ms. Edna, enjoyed talking with her, and even considered her a mother mentor.

"I'm surprised to see you here tonight, Ms. Stanfield. In most of my other schools, the people like you, uh, what do they call you again?"

"Clinical Service Providers."

"Oh right, Clinical Service Providers. I knew it was some fancy name. That's what happens when y'all go to school and come back with all these degrees. You think you must have a fancy name to describe what you do. No offense to you and the education you got, but it's all a little snooty to me, but you know I'm from the old school. Anyway, most of y'all *clinical service providers* never come to back-to-school night."

"That's true and honestly, I wasn't going to come tonight, but Ms. Carey and some of the teachers talked me into coming and maybe going out for a few drinks afterward."

Ms. Edna stopped what she was doing, propped her hand on her hip as if she needed to do that to make her next point.

"Oh okay, I see now. You gals on the hunt? I ain't mad at you; just don't get yourself hooked into something you might not be able to handle." Ms. Edna winked at Peyton who wanted to tell her that she thought that had already happened. She refrained because she didn't feel like explaining the whole Hamilton story because there really wasn't anything to explain yet.

"No, no hunt tonight, Ms. Edna. I'm tired. I'm going to have one drink; maybe two, chat a bit, and head home."

"Well, have a good time. I remember back in the day when I would go out after work with some of the other custodians. I'm too old for all that shit now. We would get drunk off drinking that cognac and talk about the crazy shit we seen. I'll be the first to admit that some of these custodians are crazy as hell, too, and that some of them need to lose their jobs as well, but it sure is real crazy with them other folks, too."

Peyton chatted with Ms. Edna a few minutes longer about the names of different drinks while helping her set up the last tables and finish arranging the food as teachers, staff, and parents filed in and sampled the dinner buffet.

彙

The forty-seven parents in the room awaited Principal Jackson's speech. They loved him, what he did and was doing for the kids. Most of the parents, mainly the single moms, loved him for other reasons as well and always found excuses to visit the school and meet him in his office. Once, Ms. Carrington told Peyton and two other teachers that Principal Jackson told her that a parent came into his office, complained about her son receiving an unfair detention, and during the conversation flashed her bra to him in what he perceived to be an attempt to entice him. Ms. Carrington said she worked in schools where teachers flashed their bras and panties to the principal or assistant principal with the hopes of getting some type of privileges, but never a parent, and this particular parent was obese. Ms. Carrington was a funny storyteller and Peyton and the other teachers left the office shaking their heads and laughing at her tales.

"Getting involved and staying involved with your child's school is what will make the difference for them." Principal Jackson repeated this at least three times in his address. "Look around this room. You, the parents, are the ones responsible for making the biggest positive difference in your child's life. Not the government, not the teachers, and not me. Sure we are here because we care and share a passion for this work, but we cannot do this work alone."

The audience was silent, focused solely on his words. A few parents looked to the floor; others nodded in agreement.

"Stop by my office, randomly walk into your child's classroom. Don't let tonight be the only night you see the inside of your child's classroom or talk with his or her teacher. Volunteer with us. Get involved and stay involved. That is the slogan for this year: Get Involved. We have wonderful partnerships with the Under Armour Corporation, attorneys FieldsPeterson, LLC, A Great Design Printing Company, Young Transportation Services, and this year we welcome Mr. Hamilton Banks, the owner of The Lucky Café and other business holdings as a mentor to some of our harder-to-reach, at-risk boys. Mr. Banks has generously agreed to donate his time and money to help our kids and we appreciate him and all our existing partners."

Peyton stood in the back of the room and smiled at Principal Jackson's remarks, especially the one about Hamilton.

That's not all he has generously agreed to do. Principal Jackson continued his speech for several more minutes and then released the parents for individual meetings with the teachers. It was seven o'clock when the last parent exited the building. Peyton remained in her office to work on her clinical notes during the teacher's meeting time with parents. She logged off the computer when she began a text message exchange with Gina.

> *Gina: You ready? I don't want to go get drinks with anyone, but you. Let's just leave.*

> *Peyton: Okay, yeah I'm ready, but Ms. Murphy and some of the other teachers want us to go out with them. What's wrong?*

> *Gina: Nothing's wrong, I'm just tired of seeing these folks today and I want to just relax with my friend*

and not worry about watching what I say. I think
I might feel like cussing and I can't cuss around the
teachers I supervise.

Peyton: I get that. I'm sort of feeling that way myself.
I'm good with that. Where you want to go?

Gina: Let's go check out that bar Bad Decisions. I
heard they have good drinks. Hopefully, we won't
run into anyone we know.

Peyton: Okay, works for me. Are you ready to go right
now?

Gina: Yes!!! Meet you in the parking lot in five
minutes.

Peyton: Okay

Peyton grabbed her things, left her office, and headed for the main door. She caught a glimpse of Ms. Edna mopping the floor at the other end of the hallway.

"Good night, Ms. Edna." She didn't respond and Peyton realized she had her headphones on, probably grooving to some O'Jays, The Whispers, The Commodores, or Earth, Wind & Fire, her favorite oldie-but-goodie artists. She walked past a few teachers who lingered in the building talking about the parents who attended the event.

Gina was outside, waiting at her car parked next to Peyton's car. "Let's go, chica. You want to follow me?"

"That's fine, as long as you remember someone is following you and slow your fast ass down. I still got to pay that red light camera ticket I got from trying to keep up with you the last time I was following you."

"Oh stop whining. It's not like you don't have the money to pay it."

"Gina, that is not the point."

"Whatever," was all Peyton heard because Gina slammed her car door and started her vehicle. Peyton did the same and managed to keep up with her the entire drive to the bar.

Bad Decisions was a popular bar in Charm Town, voted by *Some* magazine as one of the top bars in the country, mainly for its reputation for sponsoring fundraisers for people who experienced some sort of life setback. It was the bar's version of community service. Gina wanted to visit since they sponsored a fundraiser for a family of five children whose parents died in an accidental carbon monoxide poisoning.

Located down the street from the Charm Town Arts College, the place boasted an interesting, eclectic crowd, reminiscent of 1960's Woodstock.

Gina and Peyton drew attention as they pushed through the crowd and found seats at the bar's center. They ordered two drinks called the Dirty Poe, a mixture of White Zinfandel, Peach Schnapps, grenadine, and orange juice. It was a popular drink among some of the teachers in the district. Peyton slowly sipped while Gina gulped down half with her first swallow.

"Well damn, you got something you trying to self-medicate?" Peyton peered slyly at her friend.

"Hell no, but if I did I would start with that fine ass over there." Gina looked in the direction of several handsome men.

Peyton ignored her comment.

"Okay, let me hear it. How do you think tonight went?" She knew Gina had an interesting perspective. "Hmmm....how do I think tonight went? Well, for starters, four more parents showed up tonight than did last year, so I guess the district will consider that progress. It's still shameful because that room should have been packed tonight because we have over five hundred families at the school. I overheard Jackson saying something about he expected at least ten more parents to show up."

Peyton continued to sip her drink, while Gina continued to gulp and stare at her new male attraction.

"Well, I thought the teachers seemed a little annoyed that they had to be there, but who knows. I can never tell what might be going on with some of them. One thing is for sure, that little Ms. Murphy was real excited to hear Jackson speak."

Gina put down her glass, motioned for another, and rolled her eyes in Peyton's direction.

"That hot ass little Ms. Murphy needs to focus more on getting control of her classroom and less on how she can fuck Jackson. That's the thing with these young, barely-out-of-school teachers. They can't seem to keep their panties on and want to fuck the principal, one of their students or the parent of one of their students. As for the teachers being annoyed, they shouldn't be. It's not as if they don't know that this has to happen, that it's a part of their contract that they like to reference every time they have an issue, which usually has to do with doing more work. Plus, they got fed dinner."

The alcohol infiltrated Gina's blood stream and Peyton became nervous. *Okay, she's getting tipsy and I hope she don't embarrass us like she did last time by getting all loud and yelling out to any cute boy she saw.*

"Yeah, that's all true, including the part about Ms. Murphy, but I really think a lot of them are frustrated that more of the parents don't show up. Surprisingly, I spoke with a few parents of kids on my caseload before I hid in my office."

"That's cool. Anything special?" Gina stared into her glass.

"Actually, yeah. Mr. and Mrs. Alston came and met with me about Tyrell. They say he is doing really well now, not hanging out with that crazy crowd from downtown or smoking weed anymore. They said he's gotten involved in an afterschool program at Center Stage for high school students interested in acting. They had no idea their son had an interest in acting, but that he is really doing well and seems to like it a lot. They wanted to thank me for telling Tyrell about the program. They also said he met a girl there that he likes and they actually like her as well. It was funny 'because Mrs. Alston was like, 'Yeah we like her, but we told Tyrell don't fuck up and bring home no damn babies we will have to take care of.' All I could do was laugh at them. You know Mrs. Alston don't never bite her tongue."

Gina looked genuinely interested. She got serious when the conversation was about good stuff for kids. She was many things, but a slouch for kids was not one of them.

"That's one of the cool things about our jobs," Gina said. "We get to see kids do some really fun, cool stuff and make some positive changes in their lives. That's what keeps me coming back each school year, especially to this district, 'cause it certainly ain't always because of the leadership."

"Me, too. Oh, and did you see Isaiah's mom. She looked a hot mess, with that big, off-centered, purple weave, some short, short red shorts and that black tank top that was way too small for her big ass boobs. She looks like she still getting high off God knows what. I'm still trying to figure out why she even bothered to show up. She has to know her shit is wrecked."

Gina bit her lower lip and widened her eyes. She was tipsy and appeared annoyed.

"That smoked-out bitch probably didn't realize she was at the school. I swear she gets on my fucking nerves. I've known her probably as long as Isaiah been in school and that bitch *has never* been able to get herself together, walking around all the time embarrassing the hell out her son, who by the way, is trying his damndest to do the right thing and not end up like her wretched ass."

"Hey, I agree with you. Those street boys up on Winchester have given her way more powder than she can handle. She knew she was at the school because she said she came in to tell me he was doing better. Don't ask me why she felt the need to do that because we are not on that type of time and ain't ever been. I told her I spoke briefly with Isaiah the first day of school and I planned to talk with him in more detail. She said one of his friends from elementary school had gotten killed back in June when he fell off a dirt bike and hit his head on the concrete. He wasn't wearing a helmet. Apparently, Isaiah was supposed to be with him that day, but it just happened she was home and I guess sober because she refused to let him go, telling him she didn't want him getting arrested by the police. She saved that boy's life and I told her so."

"Finally, a good deed by the good mother."

"I know. She did seem sorry when she was telling me the dirt bike story."

"Wow. These kids and those damn dirt bikes are crazy. Every time I see one going down the street with some kid doing crazy wheelies, I cringe because I know they are probably eventually going to end up with body parts spread all over the street, in a coma in the hospital or in some funeral home with their mama leaning over, wanting to get in the casket. It's sickening. I don't drive behind them because I don't want somebody to fall in front of my car and I end up running their ass over."

Before Peyton responded, Gina changed the subject. She shot Peyton a questionable look and turned her entire body to face her. "So, have you heard from Mr. Hamilton, aka Mr. Dark Chocolate?"

"No, not since the other day when he was in the building. We are supposed to have lunch on Saturday. I don't know, maybe he's changed his mind or moved onto some new thing."

Gina glared at Peyton.

"You don't even believe that shit you are talking, so why are you even saying it? You *are* the new thing. I doubt very seriously he has moved on anywhere. Who knows, he might be waiting *for you* to say something to *him*. Have you thought about that?"

"Why would I contact him? I don't know what to say and will you *please* stop rolling your eyes at me."

"Just forget about it Peyton. If you insist on playing your *I'm naïve* role, I'm going to let you. Where are you two having this lunch?"

"I'm not sure, he just asked me to meet him at his restaurant."

"Hmmm, okay. How you really feeling about all this?"

"Truthfully?"

Gina shot Peyton a smirk. "Uh, why would I want anything other than the truth? Hell yeah, truthfully. You seem…I don't know the right word to use…maybe…apprehensive?"

Gina knew Peyton well. "You think so?"

"Fuck yeah, I think so. What's up?" The Dirty Poe worked its magic with her.

"I don't know, I guess I'm just a little nervous. So far, I like what I see about him. I *really* like what I see. I'm intrigued by him and *crazy stupid* attracted to him. He was really nice to me the other day in my office and so damn sure of himself. Did I tell you he stopped me mid-sentence and got right to the point:

wanting to get with me? *That shit was sexy to me.* I wanted to do him right then and there on the desk."

Gina's eyes got big. "Girl, if you had told me you fucked his ass on your desk with his wife downstairs in the principal's office….Shit, I don't think even I would have the balls to do something like that. And what are you so nervous about? It's just supposed to be lunch, unless, of course, you're planning to make yourself the dessert. Is that what you're planning to do 'because I'm sure you have been thinking about it."

"Really, Gina? And stop looking at me with that smirk of yours on your face. You think I would actually sleep with this man the first time I'm alone with him?"

"Ah, excuse me missy, but may I remind you that you just said you practically did him in your office. *Shit*, I would sleep with his ass. Why not?" She gulped down the remainder of her drink and motioned the bartender for a third.

"Well, I'm not planning on doing that. I just want to talk and see what he's about."

Shaking her head, Gina pursed her lips. "Okay, if you want to kid yourself then go ahead and kid yourself but I say if you want to fuck him then fuck him. Tomorrow is never promised."

"I know, but I don't want to come across as no ho'."

Another smirk from Gina.

"Really Peyton? You been a ho', although a conservative ho', for years now and all of a sudden you have some sort of conscious about that?"

"I'm serious, Gina. I don't want to come across as fast with this one. I'm just going to try and figure out where his head is."

Gina laughed.

"Well, I'm sure *head* will be a part of the conversation. I'm just not sure it's the head you're thinking of."

Peyton pushed on Gina and almost knocked her off the barstool.

"*Shut up!* Seriously, I'm really excited to see him and that *is* scary for me. I just can't get over how damn *fine* he is. You saw him the other day in the building. Did you see that suit he was wearing? Beautiful colors against his dark skin, perfectly tailor-made and he smelled fabulous. It's going to be a long week 'because I can't wait to see him. You think he feels the same about me?"

"Oh, here you go with that fantasizing shit. Listen, don't read anything into all this. *It's just lunch* and if you end up having sex with him, *it's just sex.* The minute you start thinking more into this thing is the minute you set yourself up for big trouble and we both know your emotions can't handle it. He's *married*, Peyton. Don't forget that small, *big* detail. I know you. You're going to start thinking he really cares about you and would want to be with you full-time. I'm telling you right now to get those crazy thoughts of yours right out of that pretty head and stay in the moment 'cause, truthfully, all this will probably only last a moment."

Peyton knew Gina was correct. She had no response, so she finished her drink, chatted more about the next day at Montebello, paid the bill, and headed home to think more about Hamilton.

Chapter Seven

Peyton pulled up to The Lucky Café at 1:55PM. The twenty-minute drive felt like twenty hours. She spent half the morning trying to decide if she should cancel and the other half carefully picking out her outfit, washing and setting her hair, and shaving all the private areas of her body, including her legs. She rarely shaved her legs.

He might end up rubbing on me and no man wants to rub up on hairy legs.

Parking was limited, but she found a space halfway down the street. She was nervous.

What am I doing here? I wonder what's gonna happen? What should I say to him? What will he say to me? She decided it was too stressful to think about all these things.

The restaurant appeared closed, although, based upon the operating time posted on its website, it was open for business. She remained in her car, called Gina, and prayed she answered the phone. She needed someone like her who had more experience than she did in such matters. Gina would know what to do and how to act. Suddenly, Peyton felt like that vulnerable sixteen-year-old of years ago with sweaty palms and heart racing.

"I would say hello, but I'm shocked you're calling. You're interrupting my binge watching of *Addicted* on Showtime. They're running a marathon of the entire three seasons this weekend. So, why are you calling? I thought you would be inside and he inside you by now."

"Ha. No, I'm sitting outside in my car. I didn't want to go in just yet. He might think I'm eager to see his ass or something."

"Well, you are, so you sure as hell should just get on with it."

"I know that, but he doesn't. What do you think I should do? Just act all professional and not ask him anything personal? We're supposed to be talking about the mentoring thing but I'm telling you, Gina, if he has on anything that is remotely sexy, I might just forget all about mentoring."

She peered out her window toward the restaurant and felt a new wave of nervousness. "The place looks like it's closed for business. I don't see any lighting and no one has gone in or come out since I've pulled up. I'm not even sure if he is in there because I have no idea what sort of car he drives and there are a bunch of really nice cars parked on this street right now."

"Peyton, listen to yourself. You are going on and on. Just get yourself out of that cute car of yours and get inside. You know what you're doing and you'll know what to say. And, like I said at Bad Decisions, if you want to fuck him, then go ahead and do it."

"*Fuck you*, Gina. Here I am calling you for support and you're kind of making fun of me."

Gina cleared her throat. "Support? Support of what? Look, let me get you straight right now. Your ass didn't call me for any kind of support. You want me to tell you it's okay to meet up with a married man, and not just any married man, under some false pretenses and do who knows what. Is that what you want me to do P? I think you social workers call it *validation of your feelings*. I call it *bullshit*."

I love this girl and can't stand that she is correct and she knows it.

"Well, I see I won't be getting any support from you today." Gina's voice got serious. "What would you like for me to tell you? You want me to tell you what I would do if I were in your situation? I don't know, but this is what I will tell you. Don't focus on the married part. You don't know what's up with that anyway. Take it from me, people get married, and stay married for all sorts of reasons, and the top three usually don't involve love. Go in there and have yourself a good time *in the moment*. Remember *in the moment*. Enjoy the food, have some drinks, hopefully the conversation will be good and if he decides to make a move, which I can almost guarantee you he will, then you decide if you want to fuck him or not. If you do, make the most of it and enjoy because let's face it, it might be the first and last time. No time to act like you have some sort of moral conscious now, you're parked outside his place."

"I know, I know. I don't know what my problem is. Actually, I do. I'm very attracted to him and that is what is so damn scary because I really want him to be just as attracted to me. If I'm going to act like a fool, I at least want him to act like one right along with me."

"Now you're starting to sound ridiculous. It's only scary if you make it, babes. He's probably just as nervous as you are, if not more. He clearly has more to lose, being married and all. And by the looks of that wife of his, she seems like she don't take much shit off nobody. I'm surprised he's willing to play so close to home. I mean, you do work for the system she oversees. Actually, she's sort of your boss."

"Don't remind me and I noticed how serious she seemed, standing there next to Principal Jackson looking like she was in strong control of everything in her life, including him. No wonder he's looking outside the house. Everyone knows that men don't like to be controlled, they want to do all the controlling, even if they don't know what the hell they're doing."

"Girl, this stuff is probably what he does all the time. Like I've said, don't go in there looking for no big love thing, it just doesn't happen that way. He's not leaving his wife. I told you about that time I was dating that married guy from down in DC. I thought he was all about me because he was always wanting to be with me, take me out and always calling. And, the sex was unbelievable. As soon as he started catching feelings for me, he dropped my ass like a hot potato. The old flip-the-switch routine. They flip the switch on when they want to be into you and simply flip it off when they don't. He never told me his thoughts or anything. His ass could have at least sent a text message or even an email. After all I did for him, and I'm not just talking about sexually, and he ended up treating me as if I was the enemy on the street. I never saw it coming and I was devastated. It was my fault, because I should have known from the outset what the deal was with him. And to think that I was prepared to give up just about everything for him. Learn from me, Peyton, and this thing with Mr. Hamilton will go all the right ways for you. Don't worry about him and his feelings. He's a big boy and I'm quite sure he's not thinking twice about yours."

"You're right." Peyton glanced at the time on her phone. It was 2:15. Fifteen minutes late was fashionable. It was time to get inside.

"I got to go, girl. Thanks for the talk, even if some of it was hard."

"Not hard, just real talk. Have fun and call me as soon as you leave; whether it's later today or tomorrow morning."

"Stop laughing at me. Bye, girl." Peyton hung up on Gina.

Peyton walked to the front of The Lucky Café. She wore black linen pants with a white shear tank she purchased from Nordstrom Rack when she spent time with her cousin one afternoon earlier in the summer. It was a fun day of bargain shopping, good Thai food and talks about the perils of dating. She decided to finish her outfit with black, strappy sandals that highlighted her fresh French pedicure. Her hair hung softly on her shoulders and she was wearing her favorite Simone I. Smith jewelry pieces.

I'm glad I could get to the nail salon yesterday 'cause I sure did need to get these nails done.

Affixed to the door was a sign that read, 'The Lucky Café will be closing at noon today for a private event and is sorry for any inconvenience. We look forward to welcoming all guests back tomorrow at regular hours.'

OMG! He has closed down the entire restaurant for this lunch. Willing to lose money just to meet up with me? Impressive, very impressive Mr. Banks.

She jiggled the locked door handle, and then knocked. In what seemed like a mere two seconds, Hamilton opened the door with a wide grin on his face.

He must have been standing near the door looking out the window for me. He probably saw me drive up and knew I was sitting in my car for a while before coming in.

He was dressed in a crisp, white Ralph Lauren polo with dark blue denim jeans, and impeccably groomed, identical to the last time she saw him. There was no silver band on his ring finger.

"Hello, Ms. Stanfield. Come in." Hamilton stepped aside and allowed Peyton to enter. "I was beginning to think you wouldn't be able to make it, but I sure am glad to see that is not the case."

"I'm sorry, Hamilton, just as I pulled up I received a call from my girlfriend, Gina. She was having a small crisis."

"Oh, I'm sorry to hear that. Is everything okay?" He seemed genuinely concerned.

"Oh yeah, crisis over. She's fine." Peyton hoped he couldn't tell she was lying.

The Lucky Café was empty—no host, no servers, no cooks. There was only Hamilton, Anita Baker's *You Bring Me Joy* playing over the music system, and the aroma of something fantastic cooking in the kitchen. Peyton bit her lower lip and rubbed her hands together.

This is it. Now I'm about to find out what this man really wants and he's about to find out what I really will give.

"I am very pleased you have made it and I have planned something special for you today. Please have a seat at the table I have prepared for us and as you can see, we have the place to ourselves."

"Yeah, I saw the sign on the door. You closed early?"

"Yes, my darling."

Darling? Did he just call me his darling? Oh, shit!

"I shut down in order to prepare for this very private and special event. I thought about taking you to the Charleston, but I wanted to make sure I gave you my undivided attention, Ms. Stanfield." Hamilton stood close to Peyton and she smelled that wonderful cologne he wore at the school.

"I hope you don't mind that I took it upon myself to just whip up something here. This way we can sit and talk and not be bothered."

What you really mean is sit and talk without someone seeing your married ass with a woman that's not your wife.

"Well, Mr. Banks, I hope you won't be disappointed and upset you didn't stay open for business. I cannot imagine how much money you have forgone for this private event of ours."

"Don't you worry your little self about all that. I've already decided it will be worth every penny."

This man is a first class flirt and he knows exactly what to say and how to say it.

"What are you drinking today? I have white wine chilling at the bar up here, but if you care for a particular cocktail, I can go downstairs to my private bar and mix something for you."

"Oh no, the white wine is fine. I love white wine." Peyton lied again.

"Okay, just have a seat and I'll be right back with you."

She sat down at a table set with a white linen tablecloth, black, cloth napkins, expensive china, and silver. Adorned with an assortment of red, white, and yellow roses, the table setting was beautiful, and unexpected.

Hamilton returned with her wine and a fruit and cheese arrangement.

"I thought you might like something to snack on while I finish preparing our dishes. These cheeses are imported. Just give me a few more minutes and lunch will be ready. I hope you like a surf and turf combination."

"That sounds delicious," Peyton managed to get out, as she munched on white grapes and an exotic sharp cheddar cheese. She downed her wine with no thought of a head rush or buzz before she ate. She watched Hamilton as he returned to the kitchen and moved about with ease as he multi-tasked.

"So, Peyton, how has your day been thus far? I just remembered that you don't care for me to call you Ms. Stanfield." His flirtatious, sexy grin returned.

"It's been good. I went to the gym this morning and stopped in at Barnes & Nobles to pick up a book I ordered. Then I went home, showered, and changed. Now I'm here." She lied again.

I can't tell this man that I was contemplating cancelling this lunch and at the same time prettying myself for him.

"So, do you work out often?"

"I try to, at least three to four times a week."

"Hmm, that's impressive. I work out about the same."

"Really? How do you find the time? I imagine running this establishment keeps you pretty busy."

"It does, but luckily, I have a very nice gym in my home which makes it super convenient for me. I have two personal trainers, Jason Williams and Wayne McFadden who are awesome. I long ago gave up the stress of trying to make it to a gym and be confined to working out during their hours."

"I know what you mean, which is why I joined a twenty-four-hour place. It's pretty cool and really close to my house."

"Well, I hope you aren't running on the treadmill alone late at night. That could be dangerous and I would hate to have to send some of my people to defend your honor."

What? Defend my honor? Now what do I say to that shit?

Hamilton sensed her discomfort and changed the subject. "Well, I hope you are hungry and ready to feast."

"Yes, I'm hungry. What do you have over there?" She continued to chew on the grapes and cheese and poured another glass of wine.

"It's a surprise for you, Miss Peyton. Just a few more minutes and it will all be revealed."

"I imagine you must cook a lot, owning a restaurant and all."

"Actually, I really don't. I used to when I first opened this place because it was just me and one other person. I was the waiter, the cook, the prep guy, the dishwasher, the everything. Thankfully, I've been able to achieve a high level of success and now I have a team of great folks that help make all this run as smoothly as it can. My man Charlie really is the one who keeps this restaurant and me together. Hopefully, you will have the opportunity to meet him."

Hamilton walked toward Peyton with two full plates.

"Would you mind lifting up those plates for me?"

She put down her glass and did as requested. He then sat down the two plates and grabbed the ones in her hand.

"Thank you."

Before her was a beautiful spread of filet mignon covered in a crab and shrimp mixture with a brown sauce, grilled salmon that smelled divine, something orange that looked like shortcake of some sort and an array of green and yellow peppers, onions, and eggplant.

He sat down next to her. "Bon appétite, Ms. Stanfield."

"Thank you, this looks delish. I'm a little embarrassed, but I must ask one question. What is this?" Peyton pointed to the orange shortcake-looking square.

"Oh, that's my sweet potato polenta. Have you never eaten polenta? Try it; I think you will like it. You know, Peyton, part of the excitement of life is one's willingness to try new things."

That sexy, flirty grin is back.

"I love sweet potato." Peyton bit the polenta. It was tasty and she smiled at Hamilton. "Very good, sir, very good."

"I'm pleased that you are pleased. I try my best. By the way, you look very lovely."

❧

Two hours later, Peyton and Hamilton sat at the table, drank more wine, and shared a chocolate brownie dessert. She opted not to have bread pudding, although it would have been nostalgic, given it was the bread pudding that brought him into her world. They talked and laughed about the political, business, and social scenes of Charm Town.

"Peyton, you are a very beautiful woman." Hamilton gazed at her with a serious expression on his face.

"Thank you." She returned his gaze. Suddenly, a feeling of confidence possessed her and she continued. "What exactly do you find beautiful about me?"

He moved closer to her and never removed his eyes from her face. *Okay, now what are you going to do? He's moving in closer and that can only mean a few things.*

"What's on your mind?" Peyton asked with curiosity.

"Ahhh, Ms. Stanfield, you really want to know what's on my mind?"

"Yes, at least I think so."

"Okay, Ms. Stanfield, tell me what you think about this."

Before she responded or made gestures, Hamilton moved in closer, inches from her face, and stared into her eyes. Without thinking, she closed her eyes, anticipating the kiss. She felt his breath on her, smelling like the sweet wine they drank. There was no kiss.

She opened her eyes to find him smiling at her.

"Waiting for something?"

Shit, he knows he has me.

Before she answered, his full lips engulfed hers and his hands caressed her face. Peyton relinquished. It was what she waited for, to kiss this man, to feel his hands on her, and his body close to hers.

The kiss was long and passionate as his tongue found its way into her mouth in an all-consuming way. Peyton cupped each side of his face and slowly explored with her fingertips as she touched his ears and the back of his head. The more he kissed her the more she wanted him. Her desire for him was undeniable.

He touched her neck and the top of her shoulder blades as her body temperature rose.

Crash! The sound was loud and interrupted the moment. The wine glasses were on the floor, along with the empty wine bottle and the plate that held the brownie dessert. With one smooth move, Hamilton stood up, pushed the table out from them, grabbed Peyton by the waist, and slid her body down on the booth seat, partially on top of her as he caressed her breasts through her shirt.

Oh my God, his hands feel fantastic. You know what's next. Are you sure you are ready for this?

The kisses were nonstop.

This is it. If you are not going to sex him, then you better stop him now or it's no turning back. She instantaneously decided there was no turning back for her.

The hell with good, common sense. This feels too damn good and as Gina said, 'Tomorrow is never promised'.

"Are you sure?" Hamilton whispered in her ear, as he kissed her neck with his luscious lips.

Peyton nodded the affirmative.

Suddenly, his strong hands caressed her entire body as they moved up and down her legs, softly and intensely. His lips were all over her face.

This is going to be awesome and something I will not soon forget.

He moved her hand to his rock hard penis and began to unzip her pants.

He is making his move and his hard-on is hard. Can I really handle all of this right now?

Her resistance triggered and without warning, she pushed Hamilton's hands off her zipper and his torso off her torso, and jumped up from the booth. Having kicked off her sandals, she almost slipped from the wet floor. Her face flushed, she was breathing hard, and her hands trembled.

Hamilton looked up at her, his expression stilled, concerned, and sympathetic. "What's wrong, Peyton? Are you okay?" He sat up and looked at her with an adorable, bewildered expression. He didn't seem angry, which made him more attractive.

Now, what are you going to say that will not make him think you are one big tease? She spoke in a soft tone as if she knew she were about to be scolded.

"Ah, I'm sorry, Hamilton. Please, don't think I'm some sort of childish tease. For some reason, I just can't right now." Peyton's face held a look of a cross between pathetic and scared. Her eyes watered.

Oh no, don't you dare start crying. Not now, not here.

Hamilton rose, straightened out his clothes, and gestured toward Peyton. "Come here, its okay."

She took a step toward him and allowed him to pull her into an embrace. The lyrics of The Bar-Kays' tune, "Anticipation," played throughout the dining area.

He whispered in her ear.

"Listen, it's okay. I want you to believe that I didn't ask you here just to have sex with you. Don't get me wrong, I think it is clearly established that I am extremely attracted to you and I would like nothing better than to take you right here and right now, but it has to feel right for you. If it doesn't feel right for you, then we are not moving any further. I'm patient, Peyton. I can wait."

She stared at him in disbelief.

Is this dude for real?

"Here, let's go back over to the table and sit down. Watch out for the wine on the floor that *you* spilled." He winked and flashed his mischievous grin.

He helped her back to the booth, straightened the area, and gave her an opportunity to calm down and regain comfort with him. Without a word, he disappeared into the kitchen as "Still" by The Commodores began to play in the background.

I know I have to say something, but what? Oh God, this is embarrassing. He's trying to be nice about it, but he's probably going to throw me out of here any minute now.

Hamilton returned and sat beside her with another glass of wine and two glasses of water.

"Here, I brought you some water. I hope it helps you to feel better. You might want to lay off the wine for the rest of the day."

Yep, I've made a complete fool of myself. Wait 'til I tell Gina this one. I can hear her telling me that I'm not made for this kind of stuff.

Peyton quickly picked up the glass, gulped some of the water, and never took her eyes off him. She knew she had to say something about her abrupt behavior. She continued to speak in a soft tone.

"Um, Hamilton, I really want to apologize for what just happened."

He placed his forefinger lightly over her mouth.

"Listen; there is no need for you to apologize. How about we just talk for a bit?"

Peyton almost choked on her water.

This dude just can't be real. I better get my ass out of here because any minute now I know that lightning bolt is coming down.

"Talk? You want to talk? Okay, what would you like to talk about?"

"Anything, darling, it doesn't matter to me. Remember that I just want to be in your presence and spend some time getting to know you. And if you feel like throwing a kiss or two my way, I'm not turning it down."

Peyton raised a brow, her lips turning into a gentle smirk. "Okay."

She knew what she wanted to ask him and it wasn't about his work with the students at Montebello.

I better start with a non-threatening question.

"So, when did you open The Lucky Café?"

"It's been twelve years now." Hamilton looked around the dining room floor.

"Believe me when I tell you that this has been a labor of love and has taken all twelve years to get to where it is today. It's okay though, it's been a great experience for me. I think my Uncle Lester would have been proud."

"Your uncle?"

Hamilton appeared vulnerable as his eyes closed briefly.

"Yes, Uncle Lester was my mother's brother and he practically raised me when I moved here with her from Jamaica. He was my father and my rock. He has passed on. I loved that man and miss him a lot and he's the reason I have been able to achieve the success I have. That man worked hard to pay for me to go to private school and then college."

"Sounds like he was a good man and that you really loved him."

"Oh, my God, yes. He was everything to my mother and me. I owe who I have become and everything I have to that man. Not a day goes by that I don't think of him and miss him. I would give just about anything to be able to spend one more day with him."

Looking at Peyton intently, Hamilton changed the subject. "Don't you want to ask about my wife?"

Oh, shit! Peyton's brow furrowed in shock. She glanced down at the floor and hesitated.

Of course, I want to ask, but I have no idea what to really ask and will you tell me the truth.

"I don't know, should I?"

"That's for you to answer, Peyton, but I'm sure you have questions so let's just get them out the way now so we can get on with whatever we are going to get on with."

"Get on with?"

"Yes, I'm planning to see you again and if I'm going to be able to do that I'm sure there is a question or two I will have to answer for you before that will happen. You don't strike me as the type of woman who doesn't give a shit. Believe me when I tell you that Charm Town has its fair share of those kinds of chicks, but they generally come with a whole lot of drama and problems, and drama and problems are some of the last things I'm looking for these days."

"Okay, so what are you looking for, Hamilton?"

Wow, I can't believe I just asked that question. Well, why not. If I'm going to involve myself with this man, I'd better find out as much info as he is willing to give up. Last thing I need is to be blindsided by some shit I didn't see coming.

"That's a good question, darling. Let's see, what am I looking for? Well, first, I like to be as stress-free as possible and to have a good time. I enjoy trying different things and exposing my children to new opportunities that will broaden their horizons. That is why I'm really excited and passionate about mentoring some of the boys in your school. You see, Peyton, I believe access and exposure is what makes the difference in the lives of children.

I just think if I can do that for my kids, then why not help a few more along the way. Uncle Lester taught me that early, to always be willing to help somebody out because you never know when you may need a return favor."

Peyton looked at Hamilton, nodded in agreement, drank her water, and thought of drinking another glass of wine. Her attraction to him deepened. *Well, the decision is made. I want to and I will see him. I just have to get to know him better.*

"To continue answering your question, I am looking for female companionship, someone I can talk to and have fun with and not worry about being nagged and haggled about bullshit all the time. You have probably already guessed that money is not an issue for me. I have the means to pay for whatever company I may choose, but that's not what I'm about. I'm looking for that person that makes me want to do what I want to do with you. I'm also looking for someone who understands my personal situation and respects that we will have to be low-key, with all of whatever it is we are going to do. You know what I mean Peyton?"

She nodded.

Don't just nod at him, say something.

She remained quiet.

"Yes, I am married and have been for a long time and I must share with you that there are no plans for divorce. But, the truth is that my wife and I have not been conducting ourselves like two people married to each other for a long time now. There's no sex between us. Respectfully, she does her thing and I do mine. We have never had a direct conversation about if the other has entertained the likes of someone else, but we just have this mutual understanding that respecting the household is a requirement. That means we each need to avoid being caught up in some sleazy scandals involving other women or men that would embarrass our kids. We have beautiful children together and neither one of us wants to see them get hurt. They love the both of us and we don't want to put them in a position where they feel they will have to choose who to love, especially our daughter because she is going through those rough teenage years."

So, he doesn't love his wife and he really doesn't want to be married, but he's thinking about the kids.

"I have friends who are married and can't stand one another and don't speak to each other. They actually believe that their behavior is not in some way warping the minds of their kids. That's crazy to me. No way am I going to have any of my kids sitting on some counselor's couch, talking about being depressed because they were traumatized by the childish behaviors of their grown ass parents. A separation and subsequent divorce now would be devastating to our kids in so many ways that both Sandra and I are not willing to sacrifice. I suppose once the kids are grown and gone off on their own, we may start conversations about what we are going to do about moving forward separately."

Wow, he sounds like he has a plan that he has been thinking about.

Peyton didn't know what to say. She started to feel this was how she was going to be around this man, never knowing what to say. He already answered most of her potential questions.

He stopped talking and she started talking.

"So, let me make sure I understand you. You are married, but you and your wife don't conduct yourselves like a married couple, whatever that means, and you aren't planning on splitting up any time soon because of the kids, but you still want companionship, and I'm assuming that includes sexual favors, obviously from someone that isn't your wife. Do I have that right, Hamilton?"

He looked surprised at her candor. "Yes, you have that right."

"And you say you and your wife have never had a conversation about infidelity?"

"That's right, not one that I recall." He lied to her for the first time.

"So, how do I fit into all of this for you and will I be competing with other women?"

He did not hesitate.

"I'm not currently seeing any other women and after today, if you'll have me, I don't plan to see other women. It's been a long time since I've been as instantly attracted to someone as I have been to you. After you left here last week, I wasn't sure how or when, but I made up my mind that I was going to see you again and soon. God had pity on me and granted me favor by bringing me to your school. I wanted to run up, grab you, and give you a big hug and kiss, as crazy as that might sound."

Did he really just bring God into all of this?

"Really?"

"What do you mean 'really'? Listen, I try not to lie and I'm a very upfront guy. I want you, Peyton. I don't know all the reasons why, but I want you. I want to talk with you, spend time with you, hear your laugh, find out what makes you happy and what makes you sad. I want to know what you are doing every minute of the day. And, yes, my wants include sex. I'm a sexual man and I'm sexually attracted to you. You are a beautiful woman. What man wouldn't be sexually attracted to you? Now, does that answer *your* question?"

Peyton felt overwhelmed by his presence.

He is a man with no limits or fears. This clearly might be too much for me. He is serious and isn't going to be willing to play no silly, childish games with me and I'm sure he's expecting me to make up my mind and soon.

She changed the subject.

"Aren't we supposed to be talking about ways in which you will volunteer at my school this year?"

"Don't change the subject, darling. There will be plenty of time next week, during school hours or after to have that conversation. Now, I have a few questions for you. First, what is your status? I don't see a ring on your wedding hand, so are you married, engaged, otherwise involved? What man has your eye, Ms. Peyton Stanfield? And don't tell me nobody because you are way too fine for *someone* to not be looking at you."

She answered his question without hesitation. "I'm not married and I don't currently have a boyfriend. Actually, I'm not currently dating anyone and before you ask, I've never been married."

"Okay, but are you currently having sexual relations with someone?"

"Nope, I'm not."

Hamilton flashed his beautiful smile.

"Well, I'm certainly happy to hear this because now that I'm seeing you, I don't want you seeing anyone else. That is my one nonnegotiable. I realize it's selfish, but it's the way it has to be. I don't want any other dude lying up and in my girl, and I want you to be my girl. Plus, my ego can't take you rejecting my attention for someone else's."

Peyton looked expressionless.

I don't know if I should be flattered or offended.

"Now that we have gotten past all those particulars, would you like to have dinner with me on Tuesday night? Lucky Café is closed on Tuesdays, so it's easier for me to get away early in the evening. I'd like to take you to Germano's, a little Italian spot down in the Italian District. The owner and I are good friends."

Peyton frowned. "The Italian District? Aren't they racist down there?"

"There is racism everywhere, darling, and the Italian District is not immune, but at Germano's, I feel comfortable, always welcomed and the food is spectacular. The owner and I met at a charity event some years ago and he is big on helping out kids in the town. He has a program where he brings in school kids and shows them how pasta is made, and treats them to a nice sit-down pasta meal. He doesn't have to do that. It's just who he is. We connected on that front, our friendship has grown over the years, and he's a good person. "You mean this Tuesday night?"

"Yes, this Tuesday and every Tuesday after that if you'll agree. Your choice darling. I want to play and I'm willing to play by your rules. I want you for myself, so you tell me what it will take to have you all to myself."

Oh really? We'll see how long that lasts, especially since I don't have any rules. "If I accept your terms, then that will mean that I'm definitely interested in entertaining what you are looking for, Hamilton."

"Aren't you? Let's just keep all this real. You wouldn't be here if you weren't. You are just as attracted to me as I am to you. I knew it when you first came in here. I propose we spend a little more time together, getting to know each other and see where things go. If after a week or two, you decide you don't want to be bothered with me, then I will stick to the business of the school, no hard feelings. But, on the other hand, Peyton Stanfield, if you decide that you do want to be bothered with me, then I will immediately get down to the business of making you feel special."

Just then, Hamilton again moved in closer and kissed her. His soft lips felt good. This time, Peyton didn't hesitate and opened her mouth to let his tongue find hers. She allowed his aroma of desire to envelop her. His soft, passionate kisses reeked of an intensely overwhelming energy of determination.

After what seemed an eternity of kissing and caressing, Peyton pulled away. "I think I better get going, Hamilton, before this leads somewhere I'm not ready to go."

He immediately released her, and allowed her to get up.

"Wow, look at the time. We've been here almost four hours. Time really does fly when you're having fun."

It's sweet of him to try to make me feel comfortable. One more goddamn irresistible thing about him.

Hamilton continued. "Listen, this time, I won't dominate your whole day, although I could spend the rest of the day, night and tomorrow with you, but I'll give you some space and time to think about my request. Let's get you home. I've enjoyed our time together and am already looking forward to this Tuesday or whichever Tuesday you choose."

"This Tuesday is fine. What time?"

"Ah, she accepts another invitation. Does she also accept my proposal?"

Peyton didn't hesitate with her response.

"Yes, I accept. I will be your girl. I feel a little funny saying it because it almost sounds a little childish."

His wide, perfect grin returned. "Splendid and nothing sounds childish coming out of your mouth. Does six-thirty work for you? Maybe we could get some cocktails before we sit down to dinner."

"That sounds good, I'd like that. And we will be talking business and you mentoring some of our kids. In seriousness, we really do need you to work with some of the boys in the school. I think it would be a wonderful experience for them and you.

They really are cool kids, not unlike kids you find in other areas of Charm Town."

Peyton grabbed her purse.

"Well, thank you, Hamilton, for a fabulous lunch. Everything was delicious."

Especially you

"Everything, Ms. Stanfield?" He kissed her again, and she succumbed.

After seconds, she pulled away again. "I gotta go. I'll see you Tuesday."

"You sure will, Peyton Stanfield, you can count on it and thank you for coming today. See, I told you this day would be worth every penny I gave up."

"You are one confident man."

"Yes, you can say that, but I'm also pretty sure about what I want these days and I made a decision a long time ago not to waste too much time fooling around with things or people that don't help me progress."

"I really don't know what to say."

"It's okay darling. Just say you'll see me Tuesday night."

"I'll see you Tuesday night."

"Perfect! Now, come on, let me walk you out before I change my mind about you leaving."

She walked back to her car and thought about her superb time with Hamilton.

No one would believe this, but I have just had one of the best afternoons of my life, even though I did back out on sexing him right now.

She was not sure she believed all he said about his relationship with his wife, but she didn't care. She'd made up her mind she was going to be his girl, they would have dinner Tuesday night, and she didn't care about much else. As she entered her car, Peyton remembered Gina expected a call from her. She couldn't wait to tell her everything.

Chapter Eight

I t was finally Tuesday and Peyton felt like a kid with a new, big, toy as she sat in her office. She thought mostly of Hamilton as she read clinical notes on her new students. In the Charm Town district, students transferred in and out of school on a daily basis. Some transferred to other schools within the district for a variety of reasons and some transferred to other districts. Scheduled to attend an SAP meeting within the hour, she also wanted to call parents. At the beginning of the school year, she preferred to phone the parents of her students to introduce herself and find out if there were any additional needs of the family. She understood that calling parents added an extra personal touch that made them comfortable about sharing personal and sometimes embarrassing family information. She followed the phone call with a letter because sometimes the phone numbers were incorrect. Peyton didn't enjoy that one thing about her job. Contacting the parents was sometimes challenging, as many changed their phone numbers as often as monthly. It was more frustrating they almost never bothered to inform school officials of the number change and the school usually found out when there was an emergency or suspension issue with a student and parent contact was required.

The sound of bells coming through the loudspeaker, which indicated the start of morning announcements, interrupted

Peyton's focus. Gina was to deliver the announcements and she purposely delivered them with animation to capture and maintain the attention of the students and the staff. Peyton stopped writing and looked at the speaker as she visualized Gina's expressions.

"All right, all right, all right, let's get this day started! Good morning and a happy Tuesday to all you wonderful students and staff of *the* Montebello High School. Principal Jackson, I, and the entire administrative team, would like to welcome you to another fantastic day of learning." Gina's voice was loud and commanded attention. The hallways and classrooms were still when her voice dominated the loudspeaker.

"This beautiful morning we have a number of very important announcements, so I'm going to need everyone to stop what you are doing and listen up."

She paused briefly.

"The theatre department would like to announce that auditions will begin tomorrow immediately after school for the winter production of *The Urban Nutcracker*. Please be on time and expect to audition in an individual and group scene. Good luck to all my future thespians. Remember, Denzel and Jada had to start somewhere before they became world famous."

Peyton chuckled at Gina as she paused before the next announcement. She heard voices in the main office before her voice returned.

"The senior fundraiser will begin next week. This year the theme is *the year of renaissance*. The fundraiser will consist of a Joe Corby's pizza drive in the fall and spring, a car wash in the fall and spring, a yard sale in the spring, a staff versus student basketball game before the winter holiday, and staff versus student baseball game after spring break. The senior class looks forward to full participation, so let's all find some way we can support our seniors who will use the money raised to help offset the costs of prom, senior trip, and graduation."

Gina paused again. This time, Ms. Carrington's voice was in the background.

"Okay, moving along, I would like to remind all students that the library has opened for the school year. Please take advantage of the wonderful books and the computer workstations that have been prepared for your use. In other words, I want to see all of you lovely, bright students fighting over a book or computer time the same way you fight over the pizza and candy given to you on Fun Friday."

Peyton smiled and chuckled again at Gina's comments.

Always keeping it real for these students.

"Okay, this next message is for all juniors: the PSAT will be administered next Wednesday and we want all our juniors to take this test. For those that don't know, it is basically a practice test for the SAT, which you will begin taking early in your senior year. Stay tuned for more details from the guidance department. There will also be notices posted throughout the building and on the junior class floor. Please don't show your poor home training by ripping the announcements off the wall. Believe it or not, some of us *are* interested in possibly attending somebody's college."

Peyton made a note to herself on a Post-it to remind the students on her caseload who were in the eleventh grade to consider registering for the test. She knew she needed to spend time convincing a few about the benefits of attending college because it was scary to them.

"Next, I would like to take this time to share with all of you that Mr. Kevin Plank of Under Armour, one of our school partners, has decided to donate a new athletic field to our school, complete with all new equipment for all our sports teams."

The sound of applause, whistles, and *woohoo* came over the loudspeaker, and Peyton assumed it was Principal Jackson and Ms. Carrington.

"We are very happy about this and a field dedication ceremony will be held a week from Friday after school. Please plan to attend and show Mr. Plank our sincere appreciation for his generosity."

Peyton smiled. *Wow, Under Armour is really doing a lot for Charm Town schools. I don't know this Mr. Kevin Plank, but if ever given the chance to meet him, I would share with him the enormous impact he and his company are making on the lives of our kids here and other children and families who have benefitted from his contributions.*

Gina's voice back on the loudspeaker interrupted Peyton's thoughts.

"A reminder that our mock Election Day elections will take place next Wednesday. This is your opportunity to learn more about one of our fundamental rights as American citizens, learn who the candidates are in the election here in town and learn why it's important to cast your vote. For those of you who are eighteen and older, a representative from the town elections board will be here with voter application forms. Our civics teacher, Mr. Hart, has worked hard on this event so let's all come out and support him. Thank you, Mr. Hart."

"Yes, we all need to learn the election process," said Principal Jackson, as he stood behind Gina.

"Lastly, I would like to remind all students to please return your lunch applications by the end of this week. It is important that we have this information and I appreciate your assistance with this task. Plus, I know most of the students in this building like to eat, so get your parents to sign and bring those applications back, and give to your homeroom teacher. This year, Principal Jackson has promised that the class that returns the most applications by the due date will receive a free trip to Sky Zone."

Gina paused again, as muffled voices, once again, took over the loudspeaker.

"Okay, this concludes our announcements this morning. Oh, I'm sorry; there will be football practice after school today. I repeat, there will be football practice. Students, remember you are not allowed to leave the building for any reason without office permission. This means you may not go to the corner store during lunch. Enjoy this beautiful day, we're glad you're here, stay safe, represent Montebello well on the street and remember that hard work and dedication reaps unlimited reward and excuses are *never* accepted. Thank you."

The loudspeaker went silent and Gina was gone.

SAP meetings always lasted longer than needed. Peyton was grabbing her notebook and student file when there was a knock at her door.

"Come in." She didn't look up, still gathering her things.

Suddenly, the door flew open and a deep, husky voice spoke.

"Delivery for one Ms. Peyton Stanfield."

She looked up and barely saw School Police Officer Barnett holding a large, beautiful bouquet of multi-colored, long-stemmed roses. There were at least two dozen white, yellow, pink, and one red.

"Somebody either really loves you or is really going all out to get your attention. Where would you like these, Ms. Stanfield?"

"Hey, Officer Barnett. My goodness, what is all this? Please put them over here on this table."

Peyton shoved aside a stack of papers to make room for the glass container and took the bouquet from Officer Barnett.

"Wow, these are heavy."

The weight of the vase surprised her as she set the flowers down and spilled some of the water onto the table. She immediately noticed the card attached, and Officer Barnett motionless as he waited for her to share the contents.

"Like I said, Ms. Stanfield, somebody *loves* you."

Officer Barnett was the last person Peyton wanted involved in her business. Everyone in the building knew he was one of the biggest dispensers of gossip. The joke was if anyone wanted something revealed, let Officer Barnett know about it. He was the one responsible for all the gossip last year that surrounded the young guidance counselor and her tendency to flash her thongs to some of the males in the building. Apparently, she flashed one of the young officers who told Officer Barnett. That tale circulated the school within a day.

Officer Phillip Barnett was a middle-aged, married man with grown children. Peyton believed he probably didn't get much attention at home, given how he spent a lot of time seeking attention from the women in the building. She liked him, he was harmless, and she admired the easy rapport he established with the children in the building, especially some of the boys who distrusted any police and had juvenile and criminal records. He was always the one giving the kids two and three more chances than they truly deserved. Unfortunately, that was not always the case with the school police officers. Some of them were brutal toward the students, forgot they were kids, talked to them using vulgar language, unfairly arrested them without warning and, at times, used excessive force when subduing a student or breaking up an altercation. Many students and parents felt their reputation was as bad as the town police department. They were also known to carry on a romance or two with teachers in the buildings they served. There was mistrust and animosity, but also some goodwill. Several years ago, in another school, Peyton started a program where school police mentored young students. She felt this helped to dispel the negative images, giving them an opportunity to connect with the students on a personal level. Most of the officers thought it was a good idea and easily agreed to participate. Unfortunately, the program lasted one year because they were unable to obtain funding to continue in the next year. The officers contributed money, held fish fry's and casino night fundraisers to try to raise needed funds. It was admirable, but not enough for the expenses of the program.

"So, don't be all tight-lipped Ms. Stanfield. Who is your admirer?" Officer Barnett grinned at Peyton as she silently read the card.

Good day, gorgeous. I'm sending these bright stems to you, hoping it brightens your day because you have brightened my days since we met and I can't wait to spend time with you this evening. Until then, know that I am thinking of you.

The card was signed: *The Lucky Guy.*

A broad smile crossed Peyton's face. Hamilton Banks struck and it was clever and sweet.

The Lucky Guy. What an ingenious way to sign the card.

She snapped out of her thoughts and back to a grinning Officer Barnett. For a brief moment, she forgot he stood steps from her. She knew he was waiting for her answer.

"Oh, these are from a guy I met a few weeks ago. He's trying to get me to go out with him again," Peyton lied.

"Well, I suppose you should go out with him again, given all his efforts and no doubt money he has spent on trying to get your attention." He still grinned.

"We'll see," Peyton lied, again. "Thanks for bringing these all the way up to me. I appreciate that, Officer Barnett. You are always willing to help. Now, if you'll excuse me, I'm late for an SAP meeting."

"No problem, Ms. Stanfield. I'll check you later and uh, don't be too hard on this fella. He clearly has good taste." He winked at Peyton and turned to leave. She knew he was headed somewhere to tell somebody about her delivery and she didn't care. Her business was her business and besides, she was happy she received this gift.

She grabbed her pen, notepad, and student file, stared at the beautiful bouquet once more and headed out the door. Pleased and impressed, she was also excited to see *The Lucky Guy,* again this evening.

SAP meetings sometimes depressed Peyton. Student Academic Plans, also known as SAP's, were for students who tested and were found to have some sort of learning or behavioral problem that interfered with their ability to function in the classroom without support. The SAP assigned a disability code to the student and was supposed to outline interventions and strategies teachers and clinical service providers must implement with the student. It was a legal document and folks found themselves in court over not adhering to stipulations outlined in the plan. Some school districts prosecuted to the point of jail time for some teachers over improperly implementing or refusing to implement the SAP in the classroom. The enormous number of poor and disadvantaged students assigned an SAP depressed Peyton and she knew alternative education generated an enormous amount of money for the school districts. She also knew there were a number of parents who received monetary benefits for having a child in alternative education.

Here we go with labeling another Black kid. Why not just change the way the instruction happens, instead of essentially labeling all these kids when they are young? Most will never get out of alternative education and it messes with their self-confidence. Those thoughts were on her mind when she prepared for SAP meetings.

The SAP meeting involved the student, parents or caregivers, teachers and anyone else involved in the child's life, such as a child services social worker, probation officer, mentor, or mental health provider. A school administrator was supposed to be present in every meeting, but there were many times when no administrator was present and someone, usually the meeting leader, signed the administrator's name to the document or got him or her to sign the attendance sheet later. Generally, someone who used to be a classroom teacher, who was supposed to ensure the adherence to all the rules and laws of alternative education, conducted the meetings. This was due to a lawsuit filed six years ago by a group of parents, represented by a crafty attorney, who felt their children had not received the proper education by the Charm Town School District. They won their argument and, as a result, the courts placed Charm Town under a mandate and gave all sorts of requirements that ensured compliance with the law and prevented other instances of children not receiving their appropriate education. It was all a joke because there were still a lot of holes in the system and many people fabricated information for fear of retribution from the district if an audit was unsatisfactory. One thing about Charm Town, they didn't care to hear any excuses—legitimate or not. They were all about appearances and they always had to be good. Never mind if it really worked for the children.

In most of the meetings she attended, Peyton found the student generally didn't want to be there, and sometimes acted out or became belligerent. The parents hardly had a clue what was going on and were afraid to admit as much. Many times, they came in and signed a bunch of documents without asking questions. It was an intimidating process, particularly for those parents who had limited reading skills or experienced trouble in school themselves. Peyton always tried to take some time out during the meeting to ensure parents understood the process and their child's progress. She tried to explain her position to the meeting coordinator many times, sometimes with cooperation and sometimes not. Her obligation was to the parents and families of students who received services. Indeed, some parents understood the process and its purposes and made that clear in the meeting, often challenging decisions made by the team and threatening to file formal complaints.

This particular meeting was for Kalia Barnes, a fourteen-year-old who gave birth to her first child at age thirteen. Repeatedly sexually molested by her biological father, she became pregnant. Surprising to the Montebello staff, she managed to hide her pregnancy and gave birth to a baby boy in the bathroom of her friend's house. Peyton never understood how her family hadn't realized her condition, although she knew Kalia was a kid who didn't get much attention from her family at home. An investigation by the Department of Child Services commenced. Based on their findings, officials arrested her father on child molestation charges, which led to a conviction and imprisonment. Peyton heard fellow inmates assaulted him frequently. When Kalia shared with her what happened to her father, Peyton had several thoughts.

Lord, forgive me, but he's a sick bastard and I don't feel sorry for his ass one bit. He didn't know that messing with little kids is a sure way to get your ass kicked in jail? Criminals might do many things, but they don't play around with people who mess with kids, especially sexually.

Kalia ended up on Peyton's caseload for counseling services to help her with the trauma of giving birth and being the victim of sexual assault. She was a sweet girl, but possessed a limited intelligence level. Peyton surmised this was how her father manipulated her into not telling anyone his actions toward her. She lived with her "godmother" who was an old family friend. Ms. Linda was a kind, sympathetic woman and Peyton always felt comfortable calling her to talk about Kalia's progress. Ms. Linda attended all Kalia's SAP meetings and was one of the knowledgeable parents who asked questions. The first time she attended a meeting, she was quick to inform the team she was from the old school way of thinking and would not tolerate any mess from Kalia or her two siblings who lived in the home with her. Kalia's mother chose to side with her father and refused to care for Kalia and her siblings. Peyton wasn't sure of her whereabouts, but heard she frequented the Mt. Royal Tavern and was often cited for public drunkenness. Kalia mentioned she saw her occasionally at Eastern Market and that she would act as if she didn't know her.

Ms. Chadwick, one of Montebello's SAP coordinators, called the meeting to order. In attendance were her teachers, caregiver, Peyton and Gina. Kalia sat between Peyton and Ms. Linda. Peyton spoke with both prior to the meeting and relayed the meeting was merely a formality for there were no new identified concerns from Kalia's teachers. Her baby boy was now in foster care and referred for adoption. Kalia didn't appear too upset about not having her baby and shared her thoughts with Peyton.

"Miss Stanfield, I'm too young for a baby. What would I do with it? I'm scared and I'm afraid what happened to me will happen to my baby especially since we have the same father."

"I can imagine you must feel scared for your baby, but are you sure you are okay with the adoption idea? Do you understand that you will no longer be able to see your son?"

"Yeah, I think I understand. Ms. Linda doesn't think I'm ready to be no mother and neither do I. We been talking at home and the adoption thing is what is best. I think I'm okay with it."

"Okay, Kalia, we'll make sure you understand everything that will happen and remember you can always ask any questions you may have."

"I will, but right now, I really don't have any. You think I'm doing the right thing, Ms. Stanfield?"

"Ah honey, it doesn't matter what I think. What matters is what feels right to you. I know you are young and may not fully understand, but this is a really big decision, one that you will never forget."

Peyton understood she was a delayed child and unable to fully understand the damage of incest. Ms. Linda confided to Peyton that due to her limited capabilities, she didn't support Kalia caring for a child at her age. She also implied she was okay with the pending adoption of Kalia's son. Peyton enjoyed working with Kalia because she had an incredible sense of humor and sweetness about her, despite her traumatic experiences. She always said she wasn't mad at her father, but did wonder what she did to deserve what he did to her.

"It's not his fault Ms. Stanfield. I just hope he will be all right in that prison," Kalia said, when asked about him. She always liked to see the good side of things and people. During their time together, she frequently told Peyton, "I'm gonna do great things, Ms. Stanfield. Ms. Linda tells me all the time."

She also told Peyton she wanted to one day attend college and help children who were sad.

"I think kids will need somebody to look out for them, to help them when they not feeling so good. I wanna be like you, Ms. Stanfield, 'cause you help me sometimes when I don't feel good or when I'm sad. I think that's what us kids want, somebody to help us when we are sad and sometimes we don't have a mommy or daddy. I don't."

Peyton and all Kalia's teachers loved her sense of enthusiasm and didn't mind going the extra mile for her. She also made an impression on the representative from the Rehabilitation Workforce who vowed to help Kalia apply to a specialized vocational program upon her graduation from Montebello.

Just as Ms. Chadwick reviewed Ms. Linda's legal rights as caregiver, Principal Jackson's voice was on the loudspeaker.

"Teachers, please close your doors and keep them closed until further notice. We are now conducting a hall sweep."

Peyton looked at Gina who nodded she was aware of the action.

Principal Jackson started the hall sweep to address the students who liked to walk the hallways, took their time reporting to class, or skipped class entirely. Hall monitors escorted all students caught in the hallways to the cafeteria to receive a one-day suspension, followed by parent notification. The sad reality about the hall sweep was that most of the students caught came from families where the parents were involved on a limited basis and didn't report to the school for follow-up conferences, which caused repeat behaviors. Peyton recognized this as a huge problem for Charm Town because the hall sweep suspensions increased the suspension rates for Montebello students and the federal and state departments of education didn't like increased suspension rates, even if they were in an urban district, with unique problems in the communities where the kids lived.

The hall sweep lasted minutes and the meeting resumed. Kalia's teachers discussed how she progressed in class. Ms. Marshall, her alternative education teacher, who taught her math and English, spoke first in her professional voice.

"Kalia is progressing well in my class, currently passing both subjects. She is a pleasure to teach, asks questions when she doesn't understand and socializes well with the other students. There has only been a few times where I asked her to stop talking and concentrate on her assignment. What I like most about Kalia is that I don't have to direct her to complete the drill when she enters class like I have to do for some of my other students."

"Thank you, Ms. Marshall. Do you recommend any changes in her services?" Ms. Chadwick sounded as if she read from script.

"No, not at this time."

Ms. Chadwick silently reviewed her agenda.

"Okay, next we will have Ms. Stanfield, Kalia's social worker, update us on her progress. Ms. Stanfield?"

All eyes turned to Peyton who spoke with passion and intensity.

"Kalia has been on my service caseload for two years now and in that time I have noticed positive changes in how she communicates and how she interacts within the school setting. She receives weekly counseling services from me, with the goal of increasing her self-esteem and decreasing her incidents of anxiety and depression, a result of trauma. She works well in session with me and is a willing participant. In fact, most days she comes to my office to check in and say hello, which I appreciate. I have observed her in the class setting and in the hallways, and her behavior is appropriate. She interacts well with other students in the building and has developed positive peer relationships. There have been no disciplinary actions taken against her and all her teachers report there are no behavior issues in the classroom. Her caregiver, Ms. Linda, communicates on an ongoing basis with me and is an excellent support to Kalia. It's important for me to note that it has been hard for Kalia to openly discuss her feelings regarding her relationship with her father. She likes to talk about everything else with me. I understand that dynamic and believe that in time and with continued support, she will be able to work through some of her hurt feelings."

Peyton eyed the room, especially Kalia, and noticed she smiled, clearly pleased with what she heard from the team.

Ms. Chadwick chimed back in. "Okay, great, thank you Ms. Stanfield. Are you recommending any changes to her services?"

"No, not at this time. Based upon my individual work with Kalia and observations of her in this environment, I recommend her services remain the same. Ms. Linda and I have already discussed this and she is in agreement."

The team saw Ms. Linda nod in approval.

"Well, if that is indeed the case, we can now hear from Kalia. Do you have any questions or anything you would like to say?"

All eyes turned to Kalia and she immediately displayed an uncomfortable posture, but was able to speak to the group. "No, but I do like talking with Ms. Stanfield. Can I stay with her?"

The team smiled at Kalia and Peyton reassured her. "Yes, Kalia, you and I will still be working together and I will still be coming to see you *and* you can still come see me."

Kalia flashed her approval grin again. "Thank you," she said in a low voice.

Again, Ms. Chadwick spoke. "Well, Kalia, it sounds as if you are doing very well here at Montebello, and let me be the first to congratulate you and Ms. Linda on your excellent progress. Keep up the good work."

Ms. Chadwick sounded as if she were running for some sort of public office, the way she spoke in an authoritative tone and looked around the room.

"Ms. Carey, as the administrator for this meeting, do you have any questions or comments at this time?"

Gina shook her head and looked at Kalia. "No, it sounds as if all is going well with you Miss Kalia. Principal Jackson and I would like to congratulate you on working hard and ask that you keep up the good work."

Ms. Chadwick kept the meeting moving.

"Okay, great and if there are no more questions, we can conclude. In summary, her academic services will remain the same as well as her counseling and transportation services. She will also be eligible for extended services. If there are no additional concerns this school year that warrant a meeting, we will convene again this time next year to review her progress. Any questions?"

Everyone at the table shook their heads.

"Has everyone signed the signature page?"

Everyone at the table nodded their heads.

"Ms. Linda, the team will need to return to either their classes or offices, but if you will wait here with me, I'll complete the documentation, print it, and provide you with a copy of her revised SAP before you leave. Will this work for you? I don't want to hold you if you have someplace to be?"

Ms. Linda appeared pleased. "No, Ms. Chadwick, it's fine. I can wait. Thank you all for helping Kalia. Even I have noticed at home that she is different and that she is trying to do good. I just want to thank you all because she has not had it easy and I'm trying to do the best I can."

Gina opened her mouth to speak but Politician Chadwick spoke first. "No thanks needed, Ms. Linda. We all enjoy working with Kalia. She is a pleasure to have in the building and we look forward to her graduation from high school and moving on to further her education. Please don't ever hesitate to let us know if there is anything more we can do to assist you with her."

"Thank you, Ms. Chadwick, and my thanks to the entire team." Ms. Linda's eyes watered.

Ms. Chadwick looked at Gina. "Ms. Carey, was there something else you wanted to add?"

Gina shook her head. "No, not at this time. I think we are all pleased with Kalia and we thank you Ms. Linda because we recognize that it has not been easy for you. Please know that the staff here at Montebello stands ready to assist you with whatever help you may need."

Ms. Chadwick was the not the only politician in the room.

Ms. Linda dried her eyes with tissue from her purse. "Thank you Ms. Carey, I appreciate that."

At that point, Coordinator Chadwick dismissed the meeting, gathered all the papers on the table, and placed them in a brown folder with the rest of Kalia's SAP documents. The brown folders represented a child's academic supports and progress throughout their participation in Alternative Education Services. Every child in the district, with an SAP, had one. They followed the child to each school they attended and sometimes a child had two or three folders. Peyton always felt there should be a more efficient manner of recordkeeping. They were heavy to carry and, for many cases, the paperwork was filed incorrectly, not filed, or lost, making it hard to locate past documentation. Gina often spoke of the district's intention to pilot a new computer program to complete the SAP electronically.

Kalia went back to class with Ms. Marshall. Peyton completed her clinical service goals and progress report, submitted to Ms. Chadwick for the file, and said her goodbyes to Ms. Linda. She then headed to Gina's office. She left the meeting before Peyton to meet with a parent.

She was in her office with three students who left the building to go to the corner store to buy snacks. Many students did this, but it was against school policy, so whenever caught, Gina gave the lecture.

Peyton peered through the door in time to hear her friend's standard, serious talk.

"Did you not hear the morning announcements? You gentlemen know you can't leave the building. It's a serious safety issue. What if something happens to you as you make your way to the corner store? You know there are always drug deals gone badly around here and I don't want any of you getting caught up in no drug boy's crossfire or one of those police chases that happen around here practically every day. Is risking your well-being worth a chicken box? You will have to stay after school and serve detention and now I'll have to call and inform your parents, like I need *one* more thing to do today."

"Aww, Ms. Carey, why you have to do that?" Jarrett Jones, notorious for leaving the building, spoke in his infamous fake whining voice.

Jarrett was a typical male student at Montebello: smart, misguided, distracted, angry, and invisible. He grew up in a house with his mother and grandmother. His father disappeared sometime before he was two years old and he knew nothing more about him or his family. His mother was young when he was born and although, in her mind, she was a good parent, she seriously lacked in the supervision department. She allowed Jarrett to come and go as he pleased and had excuse after excuse for his bad behavior. He sometimes commented she was too busy with her men to notice what happened to him. He didn't like the fact that his mother got a new boyfriend every change of season who she wanted him to call Dad. Jarrett made it clear that, even though his dad was gone, he was his one and only dad.

He always told Gina, "Ms. Carey, ain't none of them niggas my dad. Fuck them all and if one of them so much as tries to step to me like he's my dad, I swear I will knock the shit out of 'em."

Jarrett mastered the use of profanity as well as Gina mastered the use of Standard English. His grandmother loved him and tried her best with him, but she was elderly and unable to keep him occupied when his mother was away. As a result, he spent a lot of time on the streets of Charm Town running with drug boys, rolling dice on the corner, and occasionally helping himself to a car left idle by its owner in one of the nice neighborhoods.

He revealed to Gina his involvement in the drug trade and his promotion to his own operation of corners. He made a significant amount of money, which his mother approved of, but he also cultivated some enemies. He formed a trusting relationship with Gina, after a rough beginning, because Gina accepted no excuses and demanded his compliance with all the school rules.

Jarrett often spoke with her about what happened to him on the streets. One particular morning he appeared tired, scared, and distraught. He revealed he knew one of the dime runners murdered the previous night for messing up the count. Lured into an abandoned house on Joppa Street, someone shot the runner multiple times in the head, his body thrown out onto the street as a message to other runners who dared to mess up the count.

That was the drug game and Jarrett understood its power. Gina preached to him about making better choices and spoke of the possibility of him getting off the streets, focusing on his education and considering college. She had one of the teachers test him and found he performed at or above grade level in all his core subjects. To shut Gina up, he told her, "Don't worry, Ms. Carey, I'm only doing this for a little while longer. I just need to make a little more of that paper to make sure my nana and moms is set up before I leave for this college you want me to go to." Gina never believed him, but continued to keep him close in her network of students. Jarrett Jones came to school most days, mostly to rest from the previous night.

"Don't even start with me, Mr. Jones. I've already had one too many conversations with you about not being where you are supposed to be and it's just the beginning of the year," Gina lectured, her head tilted and lips turned up into a smirk.

"Okay, okay, Ms. Carey. I mean, why you gotta be so hard at the beginning of the year? Can't you cut a brotha some slack?"

"Hard? I'm trying to save you from yourself, and don't you start with that 'can't you cut a brotha some slack' crap with me."

Gina stood up and motioned for the students to exit her office and Peyton to enter. "I am done with this conversation and I will see you gentlemen later for detention."

Jarrett walked out her office as he spoke. "I ain't coming."

Gina was always firm with the students, and deep down they loved her for it. It amused her that although the students complained, got in trouble, and at times, lashed out in rude, offensive ways, they genuinely cared about her. One time, there was a visitor in the building from another school who made a smart comment to Gina in front of Jarrett and before Gina could react or respond, he defended her.

"Yo, who the fuck you think you talking to?" Jarrett's street persona was unleashed.

The visitor looked stunned and Gina immediately intervened. "Jarrett"

"Naw, fuck that, Ms. Carey. This pussy ass bitch ain't gonna come in here and talk to you any kind of way. I don't give a fuck who you are or who your mama and daddy is." Jarrett looked in the visitor's eyes, with a glare of anger and rage.

Gina, accustomed to this response, tried to calm him.

"Jarrett, I know you feel like you should protect me, but I'm okay. Really, it's okay let me handle this, please."

He snapped back to his reality of being in school and not on the street.

"Okay, Ms. Carey, but I'm just saying. People better learn some motherfuckin' manners around here." He continued to eye the visitor, shocked and silent, with his sharp glare.

"Okay, Jarrett. I'm going to ask you to move along to class and let's talk later."

Jarrett slowly moved on, but not before giving the visitor another stern-faced expression.

Gina felt obligated to apologize, although she secretly loved the exchange. It was her validation that she was doing a good job with the students. She didn't condone the behavior, but she understood it. It was how they expressed their connection, loyalty, and admiration for those they perceived as *real*.

"What's up? That Ms. Chadwick got on my nerves in that meeting, she's too long-winded, and if she interrupts me one more time." Gina stopped.

"I know. I've just learned to ignore her." Peyton sat down.

"So, what's up?"

"Nothing, just heading down to Ms. Lewis's room to do an observation on one of my students."

"Stop lying. I can tell by the look on your face that something is on your mind."

"You know me too damn well."

"Yep, I do, so spill it." Gina waited.

"I'm having dinner with Hamilton tonight. He sent me a beautiful bouquet of roses earlier."

"Ah, so Mr. Hamilton Banks strikes again. Hmmm, he is really trying to get and keep your attention. Flowers? Really? I'm impressed."

"And they are huge. I almost fell over when I took them from Officer Barnett."

Gina laughed. "Officer Barnett? I'm surprised I haven't heard about this yet."

"Yeah, of all people to deliver them to my office. But you know what? I don't give a shit. He can tell whomever he wants."

"Look at you being all confident. You're starting to sound like me."

Peyton stood up and turned to walk out.

"Nope, just feeling like it's okay to feel how I feel."

"Okay Ms. Feel-how-I-feel. You gonna be *feeling* Hamilton Banks tonight."

"Yep, I sure am and I'm looking forward to it."

"Now, you really are starting to sound like me."

Chapter Nine

It was a long day at Montebello. Peyton watched Sheinelle Jones and Craig Melvin report the evening news as she lay across her bed. They were her favorite anchor team and she listened to them detail the day's log of newsworthy stories. She waited for the weather report, so she could select the right outfit to wear for her dinner with Hamilton. Exhausted, she knew she would acquire the energy to get showered and down to Germano's. Nothing was going to prevent her from seeing him. Her townhouse, located on the east side of town, off Loch Raven Expressway, was a twenty-minute drive to Little Italy.

The ring tone propelled Peyton out of television distractions. She looked at her phone and saw the name *Mommy* on her caller ID. She always counted on Jacqueline's daily call.

"Hey, Mom." She knew she sounded groggy on the other end of the phone.

"Honey, are you okay? I almost didn't recognize your voice. You don't sound good."

"I'm okay, Mom. I was just lying down for a bit before I get up and go to dinner."

"Oh, okay. Where are you going to dinner and with whom?"

Mommy Jacqueline was nosy, but she guessed that was part of her job. She was that way all her life. Peyton never felt fully comfortable sharing her dating stories with her mother, especially since that was never a comfortable space for them and since this current story was one that involved a married man, something her mother didn't condone.

"It's just dinner, Mom, with someone I just recently met." Peyton's limp body continued to lie across her king-sized bed as her eyes remained glued to the television. They were finally discussing the weather. It was going to be about seventy degrees.

Perfect, I can wear a tank, skirt, and sandals.

"Honey, did you hear me?"

Peyton refocused her attention on their conversation.

"I'm sorry, Mom, what did you say?"

"Oh honey, are you sure you're okay? I just don't like the way you are sounding and you are barely listening to me."

"I'm sorry Mom; I was looking at something on the television. What is it you were saying again?"

"I was telling you that I think your Aunt Mary is not feeling well. Every time I've called her this week, she has been in the bed and you know that is definitely not like her."

"It's probably nothing, Mom, but would you like for me to give her a call and check up on her?"

"Oh yes, honey, could you do that? Maybe she'll talk more with you. When I ask her if something is wrong, she says no and changes the subject. It might have something to do with that no-good married boyfriend of hers. It's always some stuff with him. I always tell her that I don't know why she would want that old man who belongs to someone else. What can he really offer her? Certainly not marriage."

Without warning, Peyton felt her stomach and throat tighten, as if she received some unexpected, shocking news. She sat up in her bed cross-legged.

"Mom, Aunt Mary has been a grown woman for a really long time. If she wants to see a married man, what can we do about that?"

There was a slight pause before Mommy Jacqueline's response, which meant she wasn't going to say what she wanted to say.

"Nothing, I suppose, but I can certainly express my displeasure, can't I?"

"Yes you can and I'm sure you have done exactly that at every opportunity you've gotten, which might be why she is not talking now. Everybody can't have the fairytale love that you and Dad had Mom."

Peyton was sarcastic, but couldn't resist slipping in that dig to her mother. A part of her felt some guilt about her latest dating situation, but she also couldn't understand *how* her mother remained married to her father all those years and continued to act as if she was as happy about it as she was when they first married. She acted in that manner until his death. Her father never seemed as if he cared one way or the other about what her mom did. Mommy Jacqueline did not respond.

"Mom?"

"Yes, honey?"

Peyton almost blurted out, *you couldn't have been happy with Dad. I never saw him show any kind of love or affection toward you. How did you live with that all those years,* but she decided against it. Saying that would start a lengthy conversation and possible argument and she certainly didn't have time for either right now. She had to get ready for her own married man.

"Tell me what it is that is so bothersome to you about Aunt Mary's situation? She may be happy, and isn't that all that matters?"

"I'm just saying I think she is a good woman and is wasting her good years on his I-can't-offer-you-anything behind."

"That might be true," Peyton took a deep breath, "but we don't know the ins and outs of their relationship and the type of understanding they have. You know people in relationships have all types of understandings. Plus, we have to assume Aunt Mary is just fine with the arrangement. I've never heard her complain, not that she would necessarily do that with me."

"Maybe so, but I don't have to like it if I don't want to."

"No, Mom, you don't. Listen; let's try not to be so judgmental. I'm sure she didn't wake up saying she only wanted to meet and fall in love with a married guy and I'm sure he didn't wake up and say I want to meet and fall in love with someone that's not my wife. Its life, Mom, and these sorts of things have been happening for centuries I suppose. Maybe they are soul mates who sadly met *after* one of them took vows with someone else."

Peyton heard heavy sighing and knew her opinion didn't matter to her mother.

"I gotta go. I'll try to give Auntie a call this weekend. If I speak with her, I'll let you know how it goes."

"Thank you, baby. I know you'll be able to talk sense into her."

If only she knew.

Peyton needed somebody to talk some sense into her, but she said nothing about that.

"Okay, Mom, thanks for the vote of confidence and have a good night. I'll talk to you tomorrow. I love you."

"I love you too baby and be careful tonight," she heard her say as she hung up, jumped off the bed, and headed for the shower.

Germano's was a bustling restaurant in the heart of the Italian District. Located on a small, one-way street, it boasted great lighting and a huge black awning with its name painted in large white print with the proclamation, "*Best Italian food in the Italian District.*" There was a line at the door and Peyton immediately felt comfortable because there were Black and Latino customers awaiting entrance. She walked past them and through the front door. Hamilton called when she was parking and told her to bypass the door line and meet him at the bar on the first floor.

She entered the restaurant and, with a slight nod toward the bar, she motioned to the pretty, petite host where she headed. As she turned the corner, Hamilton was the first person she saw. He sat on the bar stool, chatting with the bartender. He spotted her almost the same time she spotted him; he flashed his irresistible, intoxicating grin at her. The mere sight of him made Peyton blush and, once again, she felt her body temperature rise.

The bar at Germano's had a fun decor. It was substantial, and wrapped around the room. The bar stools had large, plush, leather seats, which Peyton appreciated because she liked a soft cushion beneath her behind. The lighting was low and soft and contemporary jazz music played in the background. There were high-back booths and high-top tables. Flat screen TVs hung above the bar and several corners where booths were positioned. Semi-full, the place had a nice crowd of people: singles, groups, and couples. Peyton immediately labeled it a chill place to hang out, somewhere to come after a long day, have a drink or two and talk about the non-important subjects of life.

Hamilton might be right about this place.

"Hello there, beautiful." He motioned toward her and gave her a hug and kiss on her cheek. He smelled wonderful.

She tried to sound casual. "Hey, Mr. Hamilton. How are you?"

"Stop with the '*Mr. Hamilton*' bit and just call me Hamilton. We have moved beyond the first meets. You're my girl now, remember? I'm good now that you have arrived and thank you for asking. Would you like to have a seat here at the bar or would you rather we move to our table? I do have a reservation, so it's up to you."

Peyton looked around the room.

It might be fun to sit at the bar and talk with him.

"I'm good with staying here at the bar." She turned toward the bartender. "Are we able to order dinner from here?"

"Yes Ma'am, you are. Mr. Hamilton eats here with us at the bar all the time."

Peyton wanted to ask, *Oh yeah, and whom might he be sharing all these dinners with.* but she decided against it.

Hamilton motioned for her to sit down. "Have a seat, darling. What would you care to drink before dinner?"

Her body slid onto the bar stool next to him. Mr. Bartender was right there cleaning off the area in front of her and placing placemats and beverage napkins in front of them. He stood awaiting her drink order.

She scanned the bar and all the bottles. "Can you make a French Martini?"

"Absolutely." Mr. Bartender turned to walk away.

"Wait, I only want Grand Marnier, Chambord, and pineapple juice."

"You got it, coming right up. Mr. Banks, another Cîroc on the rocks for you?"

Hamilton nodded.

Peyton turned back to him, and caught him smiling at her. "What?"

"You're pretty, Ms. Stanfield. I'm just admiring how you can easily articulate what you want. I think that's pretty damn hot." He flashed his sexy grin at her.

Suddenly, Peyton felt nervous; surprised she was still uncomfortable talking with him, unsure if it was due to her feelings or his marital status. She decided to, again, start safe.

"Thank you for the beautiful floral bouquet. It was a nice surprise, but you really shouldn't have."

"Why shouldn't I have? Did they make you feel special; put a smile on that pretty face of yours? I wanted you to know that I was thinking of you and what better way to do that than to send some flowers? Get used to it, because it will happen again." He grabbed her hand. "Actually, there are a few things I would like for you to get used to, Ms. Stanfield."

She decided to roll with the moment. "Oh yeah, like what?"

He took the bait with no problem. "Like getting used to me calling you, sending you gifts, taking you out and, when you're ready, loving the hell out of you. What you got to say about that?"

"Ah, you certainly don't beat around the bush is what I got to say about that." Peyton looked down the bar for Mr. Bartender. Suddenly, she needed the French Martini as a distraction.

"So, no more to say?"

"No, it's not that. I just—"

Hamilton motioned for her to be quiet.

"Listen, I haven't forgotten our conversation that we had at the Café. Let me repeat myself. I don't want you to feel uncomfortable with any of this or me. That is not how I operate. I like you and I want to see you, and I have no problem going at your pace. You can make all the rules. I don't care. You intrigue me, Ms. Stanfield, and I'm *very* attracted to you. And, by the way, did I tell you that you look very lovely this evening and thanks for agreeing to meet me."

Wow, can this night really be off to such a great start? Is there ever a bad time with this man?

"Thanks for saying all that. I do feel a little awkward, but I should just be honest with you and tell you that I am attracted to you as well and I'm happy to be here." She didn't know what else, but the truth to say at this point.

"I'm glad you're able to share that with me. I already knew that because I felt your energy at the Café and you're here this evening. Your actions are telling me what you want."

"Oh yeah?"

"Yeah and now that we are in agreement that we both want to be here, let's get some dinner. Take a look at the menu. I know you haven't been here before, but believe me when I tell you that everything is very good."

Mr. Bartender appeared with their drinks and Peyton and Hamilton placed their orders, she the shrimp scampi and he the grilled lamb chops.

As Mr. Bartender walked off to the register, Hamilton raised his glass.

"I'd like to propose a toast: To the future because it sure is looking bright."

Peyton returned the gesture and raised her glass. "I'll certainly drink to that."

Both winked at the other as if each knew something special about the other.

"So, darling, how was your day?"

She laughed. "That sounds so cliché"

"Why Ms. Stanfield, are you making fun of me? My heart is offended."

"Oh stop, I'm just teasing. You ask questions so matter-of-fact."

"Do I really?"

"Yeah, it's like you know what you're going to say even before you say it or the question has been asked. Have you ever been at a loss for words?"

"Hell yeah, plenty of times. You just don't know it yet."

"No, I guess I don't, but I seriously can't imagine that." She looked back at her glass; eyebrows raised and took a giant sip.

"Careful there Ms. Stanfield. I saw what Jake put in your drink and it's some potent stuff. I wouldn't want you to get all tipsy and try to take advantage of me tonight."

He was right and she felt relaxed.

"That's right, Mr. Banks. You better watch out or I just might have my way with you tonight."

He laughed. "And you'd get no argument from me."

Peyton rolled her eyes and drank more.

"Seriously, Peyton how was your day?"

"Seriously, it was pretty good, but long. I had some meetings and saw some of my kids."

"I take it, you like your job?"

"Well, first let me correct you. It's not a job, it's a career and no I don't like it, I love it."

"I see. I'm hoping I can get you to love some other things."

Boy, he just never lets up and he's so smooth with it.

"Well, Mr. Hamilton Banks that remains to be seen doesn't it."

"For you, maybe. I was clear the day you walked into Lucky."

Smartass

The dinner conversation remained easy, they discussed his ideas for mentoring her students, she recounted her day at the school, and he summarized his day of running errands for the Cafe. He conducted a mock service for an upcoming catering job and two interviews for staff people. They talked sports and laughed at funny stuff in the news. One thing was clear to Peyton about Hamilton: it was easy to be with him and he was like no other man she dated. He was in a league of his own. She realized she hadn't experienced what he offered, which made her relationship with him exciting, invigorating, and liberating. As she listened to tales of the dating escapades of her friends, she realized he definitely was not like any of the men they mentioned. No, he was much different. He was irresistible and mysterious. Good-looking, great personality, smart, business-minded and a desire to pay her all the attention she craved were all traits he possessed that she couldn't and wouldn't ignore.

She asked herself, *what woman would reject a man who was fun, had minimal drama, and didn't need help getting his life together?*

They were enjoying their entrees and discussing dessert when Hamilton's phone rang. Looking at the caller ID, he took the call and lifted his index finger in her direction, indicating he needed a minute.

"Go ahead, Bosworth, what's up?"

Peyton knew he heard something that wasn't casual because his gaze turned serious and he listened intently.

"What the?" Hamilton stopped. He realized he was in a public place and in Peyton's presence. He paused, listened again to the voice on the other end, and, without an expression, stared at her. Mr. Bartender tried to approach them, but Hamilton motioned him away.

"Okay, thanks for calling, but I can't talk right now. I'm down at Germano's getting some dinner. I'll be leaving here soon and will call you when I get in the car. Don't do anything until you hear back from me."

The caller said something additional to Hamilton who responded by saying, "Got it. Tell him I said nothing is done until we all talk. I'm on it right away." He hung up the phone and dropped it on the counter.

Peyton looked at him questionably and cleared her throat.

This is not the time to be passing jokes.

"Is everything okay, Hamilton?"

His gaze softened and he reached for her hand.

"Yes, darling, of course. Just some business stuff I need to deal with once I leave here. Looks like my night just got longer. But, it's okay because I've had another great time here with you." He kissed her fingers one at a time and his easy, gentle demeanor returned.

"So Peyton, we've spent a little bit of time together, but now I'd like to know more about what makes you tick. Are you one of those Charm Town natives?"

"Nope, not me. I grew up on the bustling western shore."

"So how did you end up here?"

"I got a job with the school district upon my getting my master's degree in social work."

"I see and that's how you came about loving your career?"

"Yep, that's right. I really like working with children, especially teenagers. You know, they are an interesting group of human beings. Most people, including some of their own parents, don't want to be bothered with them, but I do."

"That's a nice way of describing them. I have two at home and they are interesting most days."

"Really? Tell me about your interesting group of human beings."

"I promise I will, but not this evening. Tonight is just about you. I would like to know what it is about me that has you fascinated. You say you are uncomfortable, but you have come back, and come back looking very good. I like this skirt. Tell me, what has brought you back?"

Peyton smiled at Hamilton as she drank her second French Martini.

Okay, what do I say now? Make up some lie that sounds good or be honest and tell him that I am ridiculously sexually attracted to him?

"I'm fascinated with how you go about doing what it is that you do. I'm shockingly attracted to you and enamored with your presence. From what I have seen, you go about your business with a calmness I have not seen before and your confidence is overly evident. Honestly, you excite me in ways I have not been excited. Most of the men out here, trying to date, have no clue what to say, let alone do. Trust, I've had my share of crazy romances and some of them may have been my fault, but I'm just tired of all the bullshit. I just want to get to know someone who isn't afraid to say exactly what's on their mind and not waste my time with a bunch of lies. I know we have only known each other a very short time, but you clearly don't have a problem saying what's on your mind. Plus, you seem like fun and I like to have fun."

There I said it and it didn't sound half-bad.

"Well, alright. I see that old saying 'be careful what you ask for' is true. That was quite a bit Ms. Stanfield, certainly not what I expected from you. What a pleasant surprise to hear you open up and thank you for your honesty and candor. We'll have to see what we can do about the *fun* you like to have. How would you like to start? I know where I would like to start, but I'm a gentleman, so I ask you first." He winked at her.

"Let's start right here where we are and see where it goes. The lunch and this dinner have been great starts and the kisses haven't been bad either." She flashed him a wink.

Hamilton nodded and grinned. "Ahhh, a sense of humor. I like that Ms. Stanfield. I like that a lot."

❀

"Thanks for dinner, Mr. Banks, I really enjoyed myself." They stood at Peyton's car, neither one wanting to leave the other.

"It was my pleasure, darling, and as I said, get used to all this. I was counting the minutes today until it was time to come and meet up with you. I know you might think that is a bunch of shit, but it's the truth. I couldn't wait to see you today and do this."

He leaned in, kissed her and she returned the affection. It was another long and passionate embrace. She dropped her purse to the sidewalk, wrapped her arms around his neck, and immersed herself in the tenderness of his smooches. She didn't want to let go. The sounds of cars passing by and sirens several streets away did not distract the moment. Her tongue intertwined with his, she began to move her hands, caressing his face, and he moved his hands, caressing her body. She absolutely didn't want to let go.

After what seemed like an eternity, they broke their embrace. Hamilton smiled down on her as he opened her car door.

"If you don't leave now, I'll be inviting you to join me in a suite at the Hyatt. I want you, but as you know, I also don't want to push you into something you may not be ready for. I feel like

I'm beginning to sound like a broken record with all this talk about I'll wait until you're ready."

"I know and I appreciate that. No, I'm not ready for that tonight and I hope you really do understand."

"Yes, I do. I meant it when I said we'd take things at your pace. Just don't tell me that you don't want to see me. He then hugged her and whispered in her ear.

"I just need to be around you. There is something about you that is calming for me and makes me feel good in a way I haven't felt in a long time and I don't want to give that up. I'm sorry, but I don't and actually I'm not sorry."

Peyton shut the car door, pulled Hamilton closer to her, and began kissing him passionately again. This time, it lasted for several minutes before she came up for air.

"I got to get going. I have work in the morning and if we keep this up, we'll be here half the night. Thank you for dinner. It's been a wonderful date and I'm glad we *finally* talked about mentoring. I like your ideas for the boys and I'm looking forward to you meeting them."

Hamilton stood back and watched her close her car door, start the ignition, and wave to him as she drove off into the night.

I think this one just might be worth the trouble.

He hurried to his car and raced across town. He had to get back to Bosworth.

The next morning, the rain pounded on Peyton's bedroom window as her alarm sounded. Sighing, she hit the off button. She was not ready to rise, shower, and prepare for work. Her mind immediately went to thoughts of him.

I should have just gone home with him last night and then I would be waking up with him right now and probably not going to work. Shit, get hold of yourself. Do you see that you are falling for this man fast? Have you forgotten his situation? He's smooth right now, but just how long do you think that will last, and do you really think he likes you enough to consider changing anything? Is that what I would even want?

She'd immensely enjoyed hanging out and talking with him. The kissing part was icing on the cake. As she thought about the kisses, her phone chimed ringing bells, an indication of text messages. She leaned over to her nightstand, grabbed her Galaxy, and saw the sender of the message. A wide smile illuminated her face. Hamilton was the sender. She quickly clicked and read.

Good morning, darling. I just wanted you to know that I've thought a great deal about you since last night and I hope you have a splendid day. Get yourself out of bed before you are late.

The message ended with a huge smile emoticon. Peyton loved it and she responded.

Good morning, Mr. Banks. Thank you for your message. I have been thinking of you also. You must be psychic 'cause how do you know I'm still in my bed? However, no need to worry, I'm about to jump in the shower and get myself to work on time.

His response was immediate.

First, I'm happy to know you are in YOUR bed and not someone else's. Can I come and join you in that shower?

Her response was almost as immediate.

Well, at this point, it might be a little hard for someone else to get me in their bed. And, what would I look like just letting you come over and see all my goodies after just a couple dates?

Again, his response was immediate.

Well, I hope it being hard for you to be in someone else's bed has everything to do with me and you would look like a woman who liked what she saw last night and knows what she wants today.

Peyton smiled at his flirtatiousness, as she responded.

Well, all that might be true, but I can't go out like that. Plus, I have to get to the school. Have a good day, be a good boy and hopefully we'll talk later.

Another immediate response.

This good boy is trying to be a bad boy if you'll let me. Remember, I'm not afraid to say I'm smitten with you Ms. Stanfield and am looking forward to seeing you again soon. I will call you later.

Another immediate response from Peyton.

Yes, please do and, I'm smitten too.

She jumped out of bed, excited about her possibilities with him, grabbed her clothes out the closet she set aside for the day, and headed for the shower. She was ready to get her day started so it could end and she could be back on the phone with him.

Chapter Ten

Teacher Development Day meant it was also Clinical Service Provider Development Day. The school was closed for students and most of the staff was required to report to some sort of training at either Montebello or another school. This day was called "TD day" by most and some viewed it as a waste of time because they preferred to be free to catch up on grading papers, paperwork, lesson planning, parent calls or cleaning up their classrooms. The Charm Town School District, unlike others, didn't incorporate days into the school schedule for teachers to have time to complete those sorts of tasks. Other districts were creative in providing that sort of time for its teachers, but not Charm Town. The system didn't seem to recognize the added stressors of teaching in an urban school district and then acted shocked when many good teachers left their positions in less than five years. Principal Jackson expressed his thoughts during a teacher team meeting.

"I have never understood why there aren't days built into the school calendar to give the teachers a mental break. It's tough doing this work and going from Labor Day all the way to Thanksgiving with no break is insane and my good teachers are burnt out before Christmas."

Peyton and the other social workers were to report to the clinical service providers meeting held at another school across town. First, she drove to Montebello to sign documentation Ms. Chadwick called her about the previous night, interrupting her thoughts of Hamilton. As usual, it sounded urgent.

"Ms. Stanfield, I forgot to get you to sign the team report the other day. I need you to come in and sign tomorrow because I have to take this paperwork over to the cluster office for review." Ms. Chadwick couldn't help but sound professional.

She's probably even professional when she's being fucked.

Peyton wasn't into giving anyone a hard time, although Ms. Chadwick wasn't always the most cooperative person at Montebello. She knew this was important, although it was Chadwick's style to make a big deal out of something small. Some of the other teachers and Clinical Service Providers in the building thought differently, and delighted in making Ms. Chadwick wait for their actions. Peyton saw it as their passive aggressive way of rebellion against her annoying attitude.

Ms. Chadwick was nonstop with Peyton about why she absolutely had to have that signature when Peyton politely interrupted her.

"It's okay, Ms. Chadwick, you don't have to explain any further to me. I'll stop in the morning on my way to my training. It won't take but a minute and I'm not exactly in a big hurry to get there."

Ms. Chadwick suddenly sounded excited. "Thanks, Ms. Stanfield. God is going to bless you. I'll see you in the morning." She hung up the phone, her gigantic-perceived problem solved.

☙

The next morning, Peyton walked into Montebello, which was quiet without the presence of students. She didn't immediately see anyone, but walked past the main office en route to Ms. Chadwick's office. Looking through floor-to-ceiling windows, she saw Principal Jackson, Gina, and some folks who looked like parents having a conversation in his office. She smiled and waved at them. Gina gave a nonchalant wave and glance, and Principal Jackson gave his signature executive wave and glance.

She also saw Ms. Carrington stand up from behind her desk with a relieved look and motioned for her to come into the office.

"Hey, Ms. Carrington, good morning. What's up?"

"Good Morning, Ms. Stanfield, you're not going to believe this, but I was just about to call you. I couldn't remember where your training was today, but I needed to reach you to let you know that a package arrived for you this morning."

"A package? Really? I haven't placed any orders for this year yet."

"Well this package came first thing and it clearly has your name on it."

Never one to move out her chair for much except for Principal Jackson's commands, Ms. Carrington reached behind her desk, picked up a small cardboard box off the floor, and handed it to Peyton.

Unsure of the contents, Peyton assumed it was some sort of promotional material from one of the companies she ordered her clinical materials. They always sent her free trinkets to entice her to buy more materials from them. The box wasn't heavy. "Thanks, Ms. Carrington. There's no return address. Hmmm, I'm not sure what it could be, but I will open it when I get back in the car. I'm off to the Govans Center for the clinical providers meeting so I'll see you tomorrow."

"Sure thing, Ms. Stanfield. Be careful out there."

She slipped the package into her bag, left out the office, and headed to Ms. Chadwick's room to give her signature on the documents. She was busy at her desk, which was full of folders and loose papers. Her gospel music played louder than on the days when students were present.

"Hey Ms. Chadwick. What have you got for me?"

"Oh, good morning, Ms. Stanfield. Thank goodness you are here. I was wondering when you were going to get here because I'm planning to leave early today. I have to drop off these documents and then I'm headed to dinner at Valentino's with my church's women's ministry."

"I told you last night I would be here Ms. Chadwick. There was no need for you to worry."

"Yeah I know, but sometimes, you clinical people say one thing and do another."

Don't let her get under your skin. She's from the old school and it would take a heavy-duty crane to change her mind about anything.

"Well I'm here so I'll just sign and get out of here and be on my way."

Ms. Chadwick rose from behind her cluttered desk and walked to the table in the center of the floor. She picked up a folder with some papers and handed to Peyton.

"Here, sign at the bottom of each sheet. You'll need to sign in black ink so use my pen."

Peyton took the Bic Fine Point pen out of Ms. Chadwick's hand, signed the documents, and placed them back in the folder and on the table.

"Done. Anything else you need from me?"

"No, that's it. You got your status reports ready for our meetings next week? I don't have time to be chasing people down for their stuff."

"Yes, I have them done. I'll email to you tomorrow."

Ms. Chadwick returned to her desk and rummaged through more of the paperwork that was stacked in front of her.

"Thank you Ms. Stanfield."

"You're welcome. I'll see you tomorrow."

The phone rang and Ms. Chadwick waved to Peyton as she answered. She left the office and shook her head.

That woman is hardcore, part of that old, Charm Town circuit of folks who came up in the struggle for equality.

She returned to her car, took the small box out of her bag, and opened. It was not a promotional item.

Inside the small cardboard box was a small, white, leather pouch with the name Presidential Condominium emblazoned in black on it. Peyton was familiar with the luxury, downtown high-rise. Inside the bag was a key attached to a gold key ring with *Peyton's Place* engraved on it. There was also a note with an address.

This key is to my condo downtown. I want you to have it to use whenever you feel like it's the right time for us. I hope it's soon. Hamilton

I'll be damned. He is a clever one.

Peyton sat in her car, and stared at the key in disbelief.

Holy shit. Is he for real? Hell yeah, stupid. You're holding the key, aren't you?

He sent her a key to his place and clearly, he intended for her to use it. She didn't know he owned a downtown residence, or at least she didn't remember if he mentioned. She, and everybody else in town, knew the Presidential Condominiums. They were swank and posh and a lot of high profile people, local and not, were owners of the residences. Peyton was impressed.

So, if he has a place at the Presidential and he has given me the invite, then I guess I had better go and use this key. I can't wait to see what it looks like on the inside.

She put the key back in its little casing, dropped it back in her bag, and headed to her meeting.

As she drove, she was thrilled and anxious. She stopped at Teavolve Café and Lounge, grabbed a chicken pesto sandwich and herbal tea to go. As she stood in line a former Montebello student, walked in, noticed her and initiated conversation.

"Hey Ms. Stanfield."

"Sebastian Irving. It's been a while. How are you?"

"Yeah, it has. I'm good. What you doing over these parts this time of day? You not at the school today?"

"Sort of. I am, but the students are not. It's Teacher Development Day and I'm headed to a meeting. What are *you* doing here this time of day? I thought I heard you were working at the plant downtown?"

"I am, but today I took off. I just got off the bus and came in here to get a coffee. I'm on my way home from visiting my pops out at Holton Lockup."

"Oh, I see. I'm glad to see you are still trying to keep that relationship going because I know it hasn't been easy. How is your dad?"

"Umm, he alright I guess, still not wanting to acknowledge he fucked up by not being around for me and my twin when we was growing up. I'm still mad with him, but what can I do about it? He sold drugs to help my mom when he found out she was pregnant with my brother and me. You know the rest of the story, he got caught up in some crazy ass bust over on Montgomery and ended up taking the wrap for some dude and getting almost thirty years. He would be out, but you know he had some scuffles in there and they gave him more time. You know how they do the Black dudes Ms. Stanfield. The Black dudes get five plus years added on for fights and the white dudes can start riots and all kinds of shit up in there and end up with only seven days of solitary or some dumb shit like that. Now, that's some bullshit, but it's also just how it is."

"I'm just glad you are working on that relationship, despite your dad's flaws. It looks as if you were listening in some of our talks."

"Yeah, I was. I may not have told you then, but I knew you were right about what you were saying about my dad. I'm trying to understand him more and I'm trying to do right so I don't do what he did whenever I become a dad."

"Good for you, Sebastian. I am very proud of you. Listen, I have to run. It was great seeing you, and keep doing what you're doing."

"Okay Ms. Stanfield, I'm trying. It was good seeing you too and tell everyone, especially Principal Jackson that I said what's up."

"I will be sure to do exactly that."

Peyton paid for her purchases and headed toward the door. She turned back.

"Come see us if you need anything. We're still in the same place."

"Thanks and I will. Take care of yourself Ms. Stanfield."

Peyton knew Sebastian's story well. He entered Montebello in the middle of his junior year and got into a fistfight his first day at the school. Principal Jackson promised him an expulsion if he didn't meet with her. They met in her office and sat for thirty minutes before he uttered a word. She passed the time by organizing some of her files and pretended he wasn't in the room. They spent over an hour talking about how he hated that his mother forced him to change schools, but she allowed his twin brother to stay at his former school. Sebastian admitted he thought he needed to act tough on the first day.

"What's your name again?" The first words he spoke to Peyton.

"Ms. Stanfield"

"Oh, so you the counselor?"

"Yes, I am one of the counselors here."

"Okay, well I don't mean to really cause any trouble, but I'm just angry and I don't want none of these niggas in here to think I'm some soft dude, 'cause I'm not. I gotta show 'em I ain't gonna take no shit. Just 'cause I'm new don't mean I'm no pussy."

Peyton and Sebastian formed a good relationship. He often stopped in her office during his time at Montebello and he invited her and two of his teachers to his graduation ceremony and party at Moe's Seafood.

"Hey, Ms. Peyton Stanfield, don't forget to sign in over here." Thelma Cottman was the director of the social workers in the Charm Town School District. She was in the position since the department's inception. Every year she spoke about retirement and every year she stood at the attendance table and greeted all the clinicians to another year.

Peyton walked over to her. She was in a jovial mood and thought about Hamilton and the key.

"How are you, Ms. Thelma? So, I see this year is not the retirement year."

"I'm blessed and no I'm here another year. Here, take an agenda, and for heaven's sake, don't forget to sign in. It's your proof that you were here. So, when I get phone calls from some of these crazy principals trying to dock somebody's pay for not being in the building, I can send them a copy of the attendance sheet. They can be such a *nuisance*. If they would just read the training agenda that I send at the beginning of each year, all this nonsense could be avoided." She shook her head and talked fast. Before Peyton responded, she called out to one of the other providers.

She grabbed her agenda for the training and signed in as directed. She then proceeded into the crowded auditorium where she saw many of her colleagues, some sitting in their seats already, and some up talking, no doubt catching up on each other's lives. The only time the social workers in the system saw each other were at these periodic training workshops. Before she could find a seat, she heard someone calling her name. She looked in the direction of the voice and realized it was her longtime colleague, Amin Muhammad, motioning for her to come toward him. She flashed a smile as wide as the bay and immediately proceeded over and hugged him.

"What's up, sir?"

"It's all good, my sista. How are you? How was your summer? Where are you this year? Same school? Come, sit here next to me."

Amin, as always, had a number of questions. He and Peyton developed a close working relationship when they met her first year in the district. He was a great social worker, who connected very well with the male students and built a solid reputation throughout the district and beyond as a premier coach of tennis. Many of his students graduated and received full scholarships to some prominent colleges and universities. He also was a proud defender of the Muslim faith and encouraged other district Muslim students to embrace their faith proudly, particularly during Muslim holidays. Within the past year, Amin decided to settle down and he got married. Peyton attended his marriage ceremony and was happy he finally found his soul mate.

"I'm good, Amin. The summer was good too, nothing too eventful. A couple of long weekend trips with my girlfriends."

"Ahhh, my sista, the old girlfriend's trip. I remember back in the day when I was hanging out with the fellas and we would stumble up on a couple of girlfriends' trips. They were always the best, if you know what I mean." Amin grinned and elbowed Peyton in the arm.

"Yes, sir, I do know what you mean. We've known each other a long time and I do know you and you have certainly had a good time during your single days." Peyton winked at him and jabbed him playfully in the ribs. "So, what is this all about today?"

"I have no idea. The agenda says we will hear a presentation on child abuse and neglect, like we haven't heard that before."

"We got to hear that again?" Peyton sounded frustrated. Every year they sat through a presentation on child abuse and neglect, as if as social workers they had no knowledge of the subject.

"Yep, and I'll be sitting here until it's time for me to go to practice."

"Hey, congrats on winning the state championships last June. I haven't seen you since our meeting just before that happened. Your kids are doing well and I'm sure you are the proud coach. That's really something, to beat out all the other kids across the state. You put Charm Town on the map, Amin, and for something great. Who knew Black kids could play tennis so well? Well, Black kids other than Serena and Venus."

Amin turned serious, no surprise to Peyton. When it came to talking about his athletes and his coaching regimen, he was a *very* serious man.

"Yes, Peyton, everything is going really good and I am proud of my athletes. They are a dedicated bunch of kids. I tell them that if they want to experience success at a level like none other, then they got to put in the work and if they aren't willing to do that, then maybe my team is not for them."

"And I know you tell them just like that."

Amin laughed. "And you know I do."

Suddenly, Thelma Cottman was on the microphone calling the training session to order. She made a few announcements about upcoming changes in the district and comments about people not submitting their paperwork to her office on time. Then she introduced the speaker who was from the Department of Child Services, who would make a presentation on child abuse and neglect reporting procedures. Peyton and Amin both slid a bit down in their seats with their heads resting on the chair backs, he reading the newspaper and she scrolling her email account.

This is going to be a long day.

Halfway through the training, Peyton couldn't resist texting Hamilton. His package was the focus of her thoughts.

Peyton: Good Morning Hamilton. I hope your day is going well. I am in receipt of your package. Thank you.

Hamilton: Good Morning and what a nice pleasantry to receive a message from Ms. Peyton Stanfield. I was just thinking about you and hoping you would reach out. How is your day going darling?

Peyton: It's going good. Right now, I'm in training at the Govans Center. We are supposed to be here until 3:00 and I'm already bored to stitches.

Hamilton: So you received my package. Any comment?

Peyton: Well, it was a surprise. I didn't know you had a place downtown.

Hamilton: Yes, I do. Tell me, are you going to use the contents of the package?

Peyton: Yes

Hamilton: Is that right? May I ask when you plan to do that?

Peyton: What are you doing later this afternoon?

Hamilton: You, I hope.

Peyton: My day is finished at 3. I need 2 run by my place for a bit, but I can probably meet up with u around 5 if that works for u?

Hamilton: It will work for me.

Peyton: Okay, I'll text you when I'm on my way.

Hamilton: I'll be waiting. Enjoy your boring training and I'll see you in a few hours and I promise I won't be boring.

Peyton: Okay, I'm looking forward to it and I can't imagine anything about u being boring.

It seemed like forever for three o'clock to arrive. Peyton hurried out the building before the parking lot traffic began. A few colleagues asked her to join them for an early happy hour, but she declined, saying she had work at home to complete. She arrived home at half past three, showered, dressed in a casual sleeveless blouse and Capri pants, and was out the door by four-thirty, headed to Hamilton's condo. She was sure not to forget her key.

She arrived at the entrance at exactly five o'clock. When she texted him that she was leaving, he texted back, instructing her to park in one of the visitor's spaces in the underground garage and take the elevator to the main level and sign in at the front desk with Mr. Edgar who would instruct her on what to do with the key.

The elevator opened and a man who she assumed was Mr. Edgar stood behind a large marble reception counter, smiling at her as she walked toward him. *Wow, this place is beautiful and really expensive-looking. I wonder how many coins it will set you back to live here.*

The lobby of the Presidential Condominiums was immaculate. Marble floors, expensive, plush furniture, a fireplace, and lots of glass with great views of the town gave an immediate impression of high class. Folks who lived there were not concerned with how they would pay the mortgage. In the far corner of the lobby on an oversized table was a display of a variety of drinks, snacks, fresh fruit, newspapers, and magazines. The lobby was empty, but illuminated a feel of comfort, style, and elegance.

"Hello. Would you happen to be Mr. Edgar?"

"Good evening and yes, I am."

Peyton noticed his formal uniform and professional tone. *This guy looks like somebody who is really proud of their job.*

"I'm here to visit with Mr. Hamilton Banks. My name is Peyton Stanfield."

"Yes, of course, Ms. Stanfield. Welcome to our residences. Mr. Banks alerted me to your arrival. I will ask you to sign in here and then you may proceed to the elevator. You will need to use your key to open. Once inside, press P and it will open up at Mr. Bank's residence."

"Thank you." Peyton paused looking at the Tiffany & Co. ballpoint pen.

Should I sign my real name? What if someone sees this and wonders why I am visiting the residence of Hamilton Banks?

Mr. Edgar noticed her hesitation. He pointed to a space in the book. "Here, just place your signature here on the line."

He has no idea why I am apprehensive. I can surely see the signature line on the page. Without thinking further, she signed the book and put the pen down.

"Enjoy your day." Mr. Edgar never erased the smile from his face. He seemed like a nice man.

The condominium was an ideal rendezvous location. It had an underground garage, door attendant, and rooftop pool with a barbecue pit. It was quiet and the residents were the kind of folk who minded their own business. It was exclusive and not just anyone could show up there. One must know someone and preferably have a key to get past Mr. Edgar.

❦

His body was exactly how she imagined it to be, strong and impeccably sculpted. His dark chocolate skin was smooth all over and Peyton saw no blemishes. He wasted no time when she walked off the elevator, greeting her with his consuming hug and kiss.

I guess he figures that if I'm using this key, then I must be ready or he's jumping me fast before I change my mind again. Some good sex would actually do me good right about now.

This time, Peyton was prepared. On the ride down, she decided she was going to throw caution and good sense out the window—even though she was raised better-and go for it. It's what she wanted to do.

She barely saw the inside of the well decorated residence before they were in the bedroom with him removing her clothes, starting with her blouse, while kissing her face and neck. He didn't bother to ask if this was what she wanted. Immersed in his energy and the moment, Peyton barely heard the music playing over the speaker system. It was a Luther Vandross melody. Hamilton had it all together.

The room had a large floor to ceiling window that overlooked the town. It was a spectacular view of Charm Town. The curtains were open, but the closed shears allowed for partial privacy. At that moment, Peyton didn't care about privacy. This was sexy and definitely beat out any happy hour listening to a bunch of women complain about what they weren't getting from their man.

Hamilton removed all of Peyton's clothing and gently laid her down on the California King bed adorned in satin sheets and proceeded to kiss her from head to toe. Her body temperature rose and her heart raced.

I can't wait to feel him inside me.

"Darling, you smell great," He whispered in her ear.

"So do you," was all she could get out. Her anticipation of feeling him inside her reached an explosive level. She felt her body juices flowing out of her.

"Your body is so warm, baby. Are you sure you're ready?"

Am I ready? What the fuck? Now he's taunting me. I've practically come all over his sheets already and I know he can feel my body trembling and can tell my temperature has shot way the fuck up.

Before she answered, he squeezed himself inside her. The feel of him was painful and wonderful. At that moment, she was convinced she was where she was supposed to be. She also realized he wasn't wearing a condom. They had not discussed this particular detail. She wasn't going to bring it up now, definitely not at this moment.

Hamilton spoke again.

"Sweet Jesus, darling, your body feels damn good."

Peyton barely spoke in between her moans of pleasure.

"Oh my God, this feels *so* good."

Hamilton's body felt a perfect fit to hers. His large stature fit with her petite body frame. He grabbed and held her as if he had been doing it for years. His strokes inside her were gentle and long.

"Darling, you think you can come for me? I wanna feel your juices. I've been waiting to feel your juices."

Peyton arched her back and rolled her eyes as she took in all of him. "Damn, you just feel so good."

"You want me to stop?" He teased her.

"No, please don't." Her voice was a whisper.

"That's right darling, give it to me. I want all of you."

Peyton tilted her head back and moaned more.

"*Fuck*"

Hamilton and Peyton made love for the first time, intertwining their bodies nonstop for two hours. He caressed and kissed every inch of her body. He massaged her back. He touched her face and hair in ways no man ever touched her. Unlike other men she dated, he didn't ask for any favors in return. He allowed her to escape in his seduction, taking great pleasure in making her body ascend to repeated climaxes.

After the final climax, he pulled out, rested on top of her, and smiled at her. He wiped perspiration from her forehead and caressed her hair. After a few minutes of pants and smiles, he rolled off and lay outstretched across the bed. Peyton lay motionless beside him, caught her breath, and eyed his well-toned body. She reached over to rub her hand across his chest and he grabbed and held it.

"Baby," was all she could say.

"Yes, baby," was all he could say.

Quietly, they lay still, no doubt each thinking about what transpired between them and wondering how the relationship would progress. Luther Vandross was still crooning through the speakers.

Peyton expected Hamilton wanted to have some conversation, but that was not his intention. After a few minutes, he rolled back toward her, smiled broadly, and kissed her on her sweaty forehead. Without uttering a word, he rose from the bed. Looking at him with awe, she found herself getting excited again, but she was too sore to entice him back inside her for another two hours.

No one will ever believe I just had the most incredible sex and orgasm with the *Hamilton Banks. Will it be this good every time?*

Shit, I'm addicted already. How did I get so lucky to meet someone I connect with so quickly and just want to be around all the damn time? And why does he have to be married? Fuck! Everything about him is perfect except that. Is there any way possible I could have him all to myself?

Hamilton walked into his closet and reappeared wearing orange Under Armour shorts and a black V-neck T-shirt. He was sexy and confident.

He jumped back on the bed with Peyton, who covered her naked body with his top sheet, and gazed into her face. She braced herself for what he was going to say. She hoped he was pleased with her performance.

"Hey, pretty girl, you hungry? Let's get something to eat." He was relaxed and Peyton suddenly wondered if all this was typical for him.

He's so calm and cool. What if he does this all the time? Oh God, have I made a terrible mistake? What if when I leave here he just never calls me again or stops taking my calls? That would be some real low-down, dirty, bitch-ass shit, but some weak guys are like that.

"Sure, what do you have in mind?"

"Well, I was thinking about calling over to the Café and having someone whip up something and bring it over to us. What do you think about that?"

Peyton continued lying on the bed, looked at Hamilton and wondered if he was going to make a big deal out of what just happened.

"I think that's a good idea. What will you be having?"

"You again, if you'll let me." He grinned, winked at her, and planted a kiss on her cheek.

"Not so fast mister. I think I need some food right now. I haven't eaten since earlier today at my training."

"All right, darling. I'm going to go into the kitchen and call the Café. Does shrimp risotto with spinach sound good to you?"

"Yep, that sounds absolutely fine to me. And can you have them bring over some of your bread pudding?"

Hamilton kissed Peyton again. "For you, darling, I'll have them bring over any and everything." With that, he jumped up from the bed and headed out to the kitchen, singing the Luther Vandross ballad that played. Before leaving the room, he turned back to her.

"Please make yourself at home in my home. I have placed some towels and bath supplies in the bathroom for your use."

"Thank you." Still in awe, she couldn't believe where she was, and what she just did. Moreover, she couldn't believe this man, Hamilton Banks. She spent a few more minutes rolled in his satin sheets, thinking about her first lovemaking experience with him.

Can I just stay in this moment, stay in this feeling, stay in this space with this man?

Interrupting her own thoughts, she decided she'd better get showered to join him for dinner.

Chapter Eleven

Hamilton and Peyton were frequently out and about town, and being his girl had its perks: concierge services at Colts park, exclusive shopping excursions to Tyson's II and King of Prussia, limousine service, private movie screenings and premium service at five-star restaurants. This surprised her because he previously stated he wanted to be low-key with their relationship. However, he made himself available according to her schedule. He also decided she would spend some nights at the condo. That suited her fine as she enjoyed the luxury of his penthouse suite. Her time there was pure relaxation, whether sampling one of his dishes in the kitchen or him in the bedroom. One night, after another incredible sexual encounter followed by his massage and dinner, she expressed one of her concerns.

"Hamilton, are you sure this is okay? What if your wife or one of your kids shows up while I'm here?"

Hamilton never seemed hesitant and always had a response. "Darling, trust me, it's okay. My children are unaware of this place and Sandra and I have an agreement that she is not to come here without my prior knowledge."

Peyton looked surprised. "How did you ever get her to agree to that?"

"Shh. Let's not talk about this anymore. Rest assured there is no reason for you to worry your little self. Now come over here and give me some more of what I can't seem to get enough of."

He pulled her toward him and kissed her. There was no more conversation about anyone showing up at the condo.

It was a thrilling and eventful few weeks for Peyton. She coordinated the school's food pantry drive and Red Cross blood drive. She facilitated a workshop on The Nonacademic Needs of Children to Montebello teachers, chaperoned the fall college fair at the Capital Centre, helped school staff with decorations for homecoming spirit week, spoke to Hamilton every day, and visited him at the condo when he was free from his obligations. She hadn't felt this excited and happy about a man since college. He made lunch and had it delivered to her school every day for one week to denote the anniversary of their introduction. By the third day, Ms. Carrington and Officer Barnett couldn't resist questioning her. They cornered her in the main office when she came in to check her mailbox. Carmen Murphy, the AP biology teacher, was also in the office, and looked interested in Officer Barnett and Ms. Carrington's interest in her. Ms. Carrington started the interrogation.

"Excuse me, Ms. Stanfield. Will there be another lunch delivery today?" She looked directly at Peyton with widened eyes.

Before she could respond, Officer Barnett chimed in. "I hear you have been feasting quite well for lunch here lately."

All three stared at her, awaiting her response, and Peyton knew what she wanted to say. *Look at you three. All worried about what's going on in my world.*

"I don't know, Ms. Carrington. Each day has been a surprise. I find out pretty much the same time you find out," she said nonchalantly.

"So, who is this gentleman? And, excuse me for assuming it's a gentleman,"

Officer Barnett chimed in again.

"Oh, I'm pretty sure it's a gentleman. She got a huge bouquet of roses not too long ago and only a gentleman would go to the trouble of putting all that together. Y'all should have seen it. It must have cost this guy some good money because they were the long stems, not those cheap shorts you get from Save-A-Lot."

They burst into laughter at the animation of Officer Barnett. Peyton didn't mind sharing a bit more information.

"Yes, he's a gentleman and someone I just began dating. I like being in this honeymoon stage 'cause the guy is still willing to do just about anything to get the woman's attention and I'll enjoy his attention as long as he is directing it my way."

"Well, I heard that." Ms. Carrington couldn't help adding that comment before she answered a call.

Ms. Murphy finally felt the need to speak. "I just love a good love story. I look forward to hearing all the juicy details, Ms. Stanfield."

Peyton ignored her comment. "I've got to run. I'll see y'all later." She smiled at them as she left the office.

Sandra walked into B, A Bolton Hill Bistro, past the host who motioned to get her attention, and waved to her girlfriend, Krista, who sat at a table situated in the back corner. Krista was her dearest friend who she met in high school when Krista and her family moved to Charm Town from Houston. Sandra never met anyone from Texas and Krista had a funny accent. She called it her *Texas drawl*. They bonded almost immediately and have shared each other's lives and secrets over the years. A cancer survivor, she was the type of friend who would fight for you like she was down on Eutaw and Poplar Grove one day and on another day stand in front of a group of millionaires and Ph.D.'s and in perfect English, describe your illustrious accomplishments.

Krista phoned Sandra, asked her to lunch, and said she needed to speak with her about something important. When Sandra tried to explain her calendar was full for the next week, Krista would hear none of it.

"No, none of that 'I'm busy' shit with me, I need to see you right away, preferably tomorrow and it doesn't have to be for long. There is something really important I need to share with you."

Sandra was nervous and intrigued. "I get that you have something important to discuss, but you can't tell me over the phone? Are you okay, something about your health?"

"No, it's not that and I don't want to get into it over the phone."

Sandra knew Krista was not one to fabricate or embellish. If she needed to see her in person, then she needed to see her in person.

"Okay, I think I can get out for a while early tomorrow. How about noon?"

"Perfect. I'll meet you at the Bistro."

"Okay, see you then."

As Sandra approached her friend, she rose to hug and kiss her.

"Hey, lady. You look fabulous, as usual. What's so important that you have to speak with me right now?"

Krista was not smiling, as they both sat down at the table.

"Thanks for coming on such short notice 'cause I know you have lots going on with all your business ventures and that damn school board, so I'll get right to the point. I saw Hamilton two nights ago out with a pretty, young woman at Blu Hill Tavern. They looked *real* cozy and I saw him kiss her hand while at the table. I know one of the managers there and she told me he started bringing her there several months ago."

Sandra stared at Krista, unsure how to respond.

"Yeah, I see the look on your face. I was shocked, too, because I know you told me he agreed not to flaunt his floozies. Well, honey, let me tell you, he was flaunting this one with no problem and she appeared quite mesmerized by him. Of course, that's no surprise because we both know how charming that husband of yours can be."

Sandra continued to stare at Krista. She finally swallowed hard, took notice of close proximity of the tables, and spoke lowly.

"Did he see you?"

"No, he didn't. It was a busy night and I was on the bar side of the restaurant. They were seated upstairs in the main dining room toward the back. I only saw him because I went up there to use the bathroom. The one by the bar was closed. As soon as I saw them, I turned my head and hurried in and out and back down the steps, but not before I peeped out the bathroom door to get a good look at her so I could report back to you. I think I left before they did because I didn't see them anymore."

"That bastard doesn't seem to care about embarrassing me. He knows I have an image to maintain. Here I am President of the School Board and my husband is a *known* philanderer. What if someone from the board had seen him there all hugged up with someone who obviously is not me?"

"I know and I knew you would want to know. I'm sorry, but I didn't think I could tell this to you over the phone, in case you wanted to talk."

"It's okay, I understand. It's not as if I don't know he has lady friends. I've been ignoring it because, honestly, I just don't know what to do. He and I have talked about this and, as much as I hate to admit it, he has been honest with me about his feelings for me and our children. He no longer is in love with me, but he worships those kids. He thinks breaking up now would be emotionally devastating for the children and would disrupt our business dealings. Hamilton is a great father and provider to our children. And he's a great guy. I can say that I've never known him to intentionally hurt anyone. I didn't just fall in love with him for any reason. We just aren't as in love as we used to be."

"I hate that you make excuses for his cheating ass."

"I'm not making excuses for him Krista. I'm just trying to be strong and honest about all of this. I don't have the fairytale marriage." Sandra felt vulnerable with her best friend.

"Do you still love him?"

"I do, but not like I did when we first met. You know, I was young and stupid for him. I'm sure you remember our dating days and how he made it just about impossible for me to say no to anything he wanted."

"Yeah, he sure did and the thing is he was really sincere. That's just his way and you know I am not really in the business of saying nothing nice about Hamilton Banks. However, I know you love him and probably always will and it is hard to be an evil bitch to someone who really is a cool person. So what are you going to do?"

"I don't know, it's all so complicated and I have mixed emotions. We have so many ties together, some you don't even know about. Maybe divorce will eventually happen, but for now, I can't see it. What would I do without Hamilton? I've not been on my own for a long time and Lord knows I have absolutely no interest in reentering the dating game. I'm not trying to deal with nobody else's thrown out trash or problems. You know these men out here don't have their shit together. Who feels like raising another child at the age we are?"

Krista held her hand up to the approaching server, an indication of needing more uninterrupted time. "Tell me about it. I let go of that Bernard for that very reason. His shit was whacked."

"You didn't really like him anyway. As for Hamilton, I am pissed about all this and hurt. I could strangle him for putting our family in this position. It never feels good to know your man is wanting someone else more than you, no matter the arrangement you have."

Krista nodded, gave Sandra a sympathetic glance, and remained quiet.

"I do want to know who this new lady of his is. If he is taking the risk of being seen out with her then he must really like this one. If that's truly the case, I want to know all I can about her."

"I couldn't tell anything about her except she dresses real fly with impeccable nails and hair. Her makeup was flawless as well and she was real cute."

"So, she's somebody that may have a little money of her own, which is not surprising. Hamilton doesn't do well with women who either don't have money or aren't self-sufficient."

"Well, by the looks of things that night, he is doing *real* well with this one."

Peyton decided to wander down to the gymnasium where the student-staff basketball game took place. She stopped at the concessions and grabbed a bag of popcorn. On her way into the gym, she encountered Principal Jackson chatting with some of the students.

"Hey, Ms. Stanfield. Nice to see you could make it out your office and spend some time with us."

Peyton looked at Principal Jackson, at the students, and then back at him. She decided to hold her thoughts.

Speaking of spending time, you seem to be spending a lot of time with a certain teacher in the building.

"Yeah, I thought I would take a break, check out the game for a bit, and go back to work. My quarter clinical summary reports are due soon."

"Hey, I'm glad I'm seeing you because I wanted to ask you how things are working out with Hamilton Banks. Has he started mentoring any students yet?"

No, not yet, but he has started mentoring me. Peyton smiled at her thoughts.

"Did I say something funny?" Principal Jackson looked perplexed.

"Oh no, I just had a thought flash across my mind. Actually, he is scheduled to meet with Isaiah Washington and a few other students I am considering within the next week."

Principal Jackson looked pleased. "Isaiah's an excellent choice. I was just talking with him the other day about possible college choices. He's starting to talk that college talk."

"Yes, he is and Mr. Banks will probably be a great mentor and influence for him. Plus, he knows a number of people in Charm Town that might be willing to help with whatever is needed, not just for Isaiah, but for all the boys."

Peyton's thoughts took over again. *Because he sure has been mentoring my ass just fine.*

"Okay, great. Please keep me in the loop of information. Do you have any other students identified?"

"Yes, currently, I have identified four additional students: Shemar Jacobs, Terrence Harris, Jerome Wilson, and Dewade Saunders. I was also considering Jarrett Jones but I'm not sure he would be receptive."

"Perfect choices. As for Mr. Jones, you may want to speak with Ms. Carey about him. You know he's her pet project."

Peyton laughed. "Yes he is, but I think she enjoys the challenge."

"When I see the others, I will encourage them to engage with Mr. Banks and take full advantage of what he is offering."

I couldn't agree with you more. The thought was spine tingling.

It was the first school board meeting of the school year and the rain pounded relentlessly on the roof, sounding like a herd of horses stampeding over her head, it was so loud. Sandra stood in front of the mirror of her personal bathroom in the board office suite and smoothed out the ginger-toned foundation on her face. Her day was busy: mother-daughter breakfast at Maysa's school, meetings with accountants and lawyers to discuss the district's budget deficits and surpluses, lunch with the principal consortium group, a briefing with the private investigator she hired to follow Hamilton and identify his new lover and now preparing for the evening's board meeting. Sandra maneuvered through the parking lot traffic to make her way down Interstate 92 toward central offices at South Avenue. She arrived to the garage with thirty minutes to spare before show time, which was what this was to her. She secretly loathed these meetings and wondered how much longer she could do this "one more favor" for Hamilton. After all, he has once again humiliated her, but this time by carrying on an affair with a social worker at one of the schools in her district. Newly elected as the president of the school board and her selfish husband had the audacity to carry on with someone employed by the organization she oversaw. To her, that was Hamilton, always caring about nobody but himself. This one's name was Peyton Stanfield and she knew absolutely nothing about her, but she knew this affair was different because he took her to Blu Hill. It was their spot and the first place he took her on their first date and she remembered the flank steak and sweet potato polenta he ordered for her. She was appalled he had the courage to take another woman to their special place. Every couple had a special place and Hamilton was sloppy with his personal relationships. It concerned Sandra and she hoped he hadn't shared all the business dealings with this young tramp, Peyton.

She recalled the conversation with the investigator.

"Ms. Banks, the woman who is taking up a lot of your husband's time is named Peyton Stanfield. She's a social worker at Montebello High School. She lives alone on the east side of town. She drives a Lexus LS and likes to shop in nice boutiques. I tried to look up her history. She's not from Baltimore, but on the shore. She has no criminal record, but there was a recordation of her receiving a sizable monetary settlement from an estate, my guess a relative, so she seems to be set financially. She owns properties here, South Carolina and Alabama. She and Hamilton met at the downtown condo three times this past week and she stayed the night each time. The doorman seemed familiar with her because they chatted for a few minutes each time she visited. She used a key to enter the elevator. Since I've been following them, they've gone to dinner at Salt Tavern, Annabel Lee Tavern,

Fleming's Prime Steakhouse and Wine Bar and they also went to the Café. They always pick tables either in a private area or in the back of the restaurant. At Salt and Annabel Lee, they spent time in the kitchen talking with the chef. He has kissed her publicly seven times."

Thank goodness for Krista and her willingness to alert me to this affair. She knows plenty about this marriage, but she doesn't know everything and I'm fucking pissed he thinks he's smarter than I am. This mothafucka actually thinks I won't find out he's been fucking this girl at the Café and in the downtown condo, the condo my family's money was used to purchase. I wonder if he has gotten the balls to take her to our apartment in Manhattan. He better not have, or even told her about that place. If the secret was ever to get out and an investigation ensues, that place would be discovered and how we got the cash to pay for it will definitely be of interest. No, he couldn't be that stupid, or could he? Pussy has a way of making men very stupid.

Constance, Sandra's board assistant, burst into the bathroom, and interrupted her thoughts.

"Mrs. Banks!" she let out in her high-pitched, sometimes panicked voice. "The photographer and videographer have arrived. It looks like it will be a light night. Only about fifteen parents have signed in thus far and I don't think we will get many more. The weather sucks too badly and there is nothing juicy on the calendar, no protests, or contentious hearings, it's too early in the school year."

"Okay, Constance, thanks for the update."

Sandra never looked away from the mirror, applied her midnight black mascara, and still thought about her husband having sex with this other woman, his latest conquest. She wondered if this one knew she was one of a long line of naïve participants in his game. As angry as she was, she was equally hurt, although she never admitted such to him. In the end, it all became an arrangement, something she agreed to do with him. They long ago realized their marriage was no love fest, but the opportunity brought to them more than justified their continued union.

Not having received a return response, Constance turned to walk away when Sandra looked up from the mirror.

"Constance, any more information on Peyton Stanfield?" Once her conversation with the investigator ended, she immediately phoned Constance to have her find any information on Peyton.

"Not yet, only what I have told you earlier on the phone. She works at Montebello High School, been there three years. When I pulled her work evaluations, she received proficient with notations regarding her superb clinical skills in working with children and families."

Constance stated all of this in an even higher-pitched voice.

"She's not married and she doesn't have any kids, according to her benefits package. No disciplinary actions against her. My friend, Esther, happens to be the school secretary over there and I called her after you asked me to find out about her. You probably remember me talking about my friend Esther who goes with me to the Five Mile House and sometimes we go to the Haven. She didn't have anything bad to say. She said she is well-liked by most of the staff, especially the male staff. Not because she's loose or anything, but because they find her attractive and friendly. Apparently, she has some new person in her life because Esther said she's been getting flowers and lunch delivered to her at the school. Some of the young, Black, female teachers act like they don't like her, but Esther said that's because they are jealous of how she carries herself. She works well with the kids and parents over there and you know they aren't an easy task.

Worse thing Esther said about her was that she's late for work a lot. That's it, Mrs. Banks. From what I can tell from what Esther said, she seems to be a decent person."

"Decent my ass" Sandra retorted. "Even if she doesn't know me, she should know Hamilton is married, which means she should know to leave his ass alone. No worries, cause the day is coming real soon when little Miss Peyton and I are going to have a nice little chat. I'll be damned if she's going to fuck up my money."

Constance heard all this sort of talk before. She didn't know this was about Hamilton, but she wasn't surprised. This was not his first turn at the rodeo of women.

"Okay, Sandra. Let's go." She reached for Sandra's arm and pulled her to the door. "You don't need any more makeup. You're always the most beautiful woman in the place."

Sandra appreciated Constance's compliments and constant willingness to make her feel uplifted, even if at her expense. She made a mental note to send her one of those fruit or baked goods bouquets she saw online. That would surely make her day. She was also sure she would probably take it home to share with her grandchildren she raised because her only son, hospitalized for severe depression, resided in a facility in Mechanicsville.

As they walked down the hallway to the boardroom, Sandra reminded Constance of documents she needed to review in the next week.

"Constance, please remember to get me that report of all the Title A funding that was received by the schools this school year and the funds that is slated to be received next school year. I need to do some comparative analysis. I will also need the printout of which families in the district received benefits from their child's disability code."

"I thought all the Title A money reports were being analyzed by the new Federal Programs Office on the third floor?"

"They are, but until they get their act together, I need to conduct a review as well to make sure there are no problems."

"Okay, but you know that is just putting a whole bunch of extra work on your plate and let me remind you that you are always complaining of having a lot of already existing work."

Sandra glanced over at Constance and rolled her eyes. "Just pull the reports Constance and also set up a meeting with Arnold Whetstine."

"The government's accountant in the finance office?"

"Yes, Constance, that would be the one."

Constance glanced at Sandra with a look of inquisition. "Okay, Mrs. Banks. I'll take care of that as well."

"Thank you."

"Calling the meeting to order, I would like to thank our guests and parents for coming out in this weather for our first meeting of this school year to share an opinion on the important work of the board. Without your participation and input, our jobs would be much harder to do. We are hopeful this school year will be the best ever." Sandra gave the same speech at the first board meeting of every school year.

"Our first agenda item is the approval of new teachers and administrators for this school year, followed by a discussion of the upcoming change in standardized assessment testing, school renovations, alternative education funding, and the proposed school budget for the next year. We will conclude with any comments from the public and I believe there are at least three registered public comments." Sandra looked up and smirked at the visitors. "Hopefully, we will not be here all night."

Her words were interrupted by a disturbance in the back, muffled voices that became loud and clear.

"Fuck Charm Town schools. Y'all ain't never done nothing good for kids. All you do is worry about your own asses and not what's best for these kids. These schools are hot as hell, have no air-conditioning, but here you all sit in your fancy pretty offices with air conditioning. Why don't you go out and sit in one of those hot ass buildings you call schools?" The voice was from a tall, stocky, man who stood in the back, yelling.

Sandra was unmoved by the commotion.

Damn, I was hoping to get through the meeting without any shit. He needs to sit his big ass down and shut the fuck up.

She continued to look forward and made minimal facial expressions or gestures, aware of the camera's presence.

Security moved toward him, but he kept talking.

"And I want to know what happens with all the money you supposed to have. My kid's teachers keep telling him and his class that there ain't no money for their art and science projects. And, my daughter came home yesterday saying her bathroom has no toilet paper or soap and she keep telling her principal. Her field trip was cancelled last school year because there was no money to pay for the bus. And where's the money you promised for the afterschool programs? That's what we need to be talking about on an agenda. Fuck your agenda, lady. Why don't you come down here with all us parents and see what is really going on?"

Security reached the spectator as he continued to shout at the crowd.

"All you motherfuckers need to do something about these schools and the shady people who run them." His voice trailed off as the two school police officers escorted him out the room.

Sandra continued to look unfazed as she spoke to the camera operator.

"Sir, are you able to edit that portion of the meeting out?"

"Sure thing, Madam Chairperson. It's no problem."

"Thank you." Sandra looked around the room. "Ladies and gentleman, I apologize for the disruption. Now, let's get on with our agenda items." Looking at her watch, she realized Hamilton was probably in his meeting.

The meeting took place in the downstairs bar of The Lucky Café. Hamilton always liked to have the meetings at a location that was in his control. He started and stopped the meeting whenever he chose and was in full control of those that attended. No one could just "happen" to show up. In the room were Hamilton, Mr. Edgar, Officer Barnett, Arnold Whetstine, and Lakya Grimes, whose son, Laquan, was a student in Charm Town schools. They resided in the 20242 zip code. The group came together an hour earlier and enjoyed cocktails and dinner. The Lucky Café was the favorite meeting location of the group because they knew there were two things: good food and good drink.

Hamilton interrupted the casual conversation.

"Okay, let's get down to business. Mr. Edgar, how much do we have?"

Mr. Edgar read from charts he prepared.

"Let's see. In June, you know we collected our usual amount. In August, we collected slightly less than June and just last week the collection was fifty percent below the amount collected at the same time last year."

Hamilton flashed a surprised and annoyed expression. "Why so low and why am I just hearing about this drop in number?"

Edgar looked nervous for no reason. "Well, Hamilton, you must remember that Ms. Gaither has been out sick and wasn't able to make it around to everyone."

Hamilton's face relaxed and turned to Ms. Gaither.

"That's right. I'm sorry; my mind has been occupied lately. I did hear about your illness, Lakya. How are you feeling?"

"I'm great, especially since now I'm here. It was nothing too serious anyway. Just some fibroids I had to get removed. That Black woman's archenemy. You'll be happy to know that I'm back on my game."

Lakya Grimes was a lifetime resident of the 20242 Zip Code in Charm Town and went to school in Charm Town. A smart girl, she received mostly A's and B's in high school. She aspired to attend college, but in her senior year, she was broke and wanted the entire line of Gap Fashions and to attend the prom. She made the choice to be a "hold girl" for one of the local drug rings. Her exposure to thousands of dollars from one night's work convinced her to move to the other side. She stopped going to school regularly and started hiding drugs and cash. She also tried a run in the escort business. A beautiful face and body that avoided using drugs or alcohol, she dabbled in the lifestyle of some rich, married men who wanted company. Most were from out-of-town, but a few were local. Her usual rendezvous spot was the Poet's Inn, an upscale bed and breakfast. She couldn't believe the number of men who simply wanted companionship, someone to talk to, watch movies, and down shots of tequila and vodka. She once boasted she made twenty thousand cash in one month. She eventually abandoned the lifestyle to raise her son by a man who was an ex-Navy sailor and made great money selling used cars for cash to people with no credit. He loved her and provided for her and their son. She tried to return to her studies, but always found a reason to drop out, her tastes for fast money more alluring. Known as *Miss Kee-ya* to the kids on the block and liked by most, she knew the families in the area, who was sexing whom, whose daddy was locked up, dead or just gone, who picked up the latest drug habit and who was about to be kicked out their house for not paying the rent man. She made friends with the cops on the beat and usually knew when a bust was on the horizon. She was the perfect lookout. She met Hamilton early one Sunday morning at Lucky when Officer Barnett suggested they meet. A long time ago, she dated his brother and his family still fumed over the fact they never married.

"That's what I love to hear and I'm glad it wasn't anything too serious. We can't take our health for granted because tomorrow is not guaranteed. Officer Barnett, anything going on down at headquarters that I need to know about?"

Officer Barnett sat down his glass of Johnny Walker Black. "No, sir. Everything is good on that front. All calm and quiet."

"Perfect. Okay, Arnold, your turn. Are we keeping our addition and subtraction straight?" Hamilton chuckled. He liked to poke fun at Arnold. He appeared to be a nerd, but he was an extremely intelligent man and Hamilton was initially surprised when Mr. Edgar shared he would be an excellent addition to the team. He and Arnold were childhood friends from Charm Town and Mr. Edgar trusted him with his every secret. Turned out, Arnold was not nerdy. He regularly enjoyed expensive cocktails and good times with several different women.

"The addition and subtraction is all straight. I'll be looking to change our system soon. I don't want to keep doing the same thing. It might create some unwanted attention."

Hamilton fired back in his most serious tone. "We certainly don't need any extra attention so do whatever is necessary. I trust you Whetstine. Not at first, but my man Edgar says you are the best and I believe everything he tells me."

Arnold smiled and nodded in Hamilton's direction.

Hamilton paused and smiled back at everyone in the group.

"Now, this is what I like to hear. I hate to talk business and shut things down, but I have to go. Edgar has your money. This was a good meeting and I'll see you all next month. Oh, and let me remind you that no one, and I mean no one, can know of this meeting or any of our other meetings taking place. I know I don't have to remind any of you of what is at stake."

All nodded in agreement.

Chapter Twelve

"Tynisha Coleman, I'll repeat myself. Why are you in this main office for the third time today?" asked Ms. Carrington, the Montebello High School secretary, from behind her desk. Her desk faced the doorway and each morning she abruptly stopped students as soon as they entered the main office suite, asked them if they had a pass, where they were going, and who they needed to see.

"I'm looking for Principal Jackson. He said he would help me with my SAT stuff."

"Tynisha, you know full well Principal Jackson is downstairs doing cafeteria duty, which is where you are supposed to be."

"I know, Ms. Carrington, but I don't like going in that cafeteria. It smells funny, the food sucks, and the cafeteria ladies are mean and will embarrass you if your card doesn't work. I swear I'll smack one of those b's if they keep getting smart with me. I'm telling you. It ain't right to make fun of kid's money situations. Some kids can't help if their peoples don't have the money." Tynisha was in her usual animated stance, with her hands on her hips.

"Tynisha, I need for you to just go where you are supposed to be. I can't do this every day with you. You know the main office must stay clear of students. Why don't you go to your guidance counselor's office for the rest of the lunch period?"

"Ms. Carrington, you know that woman be acting funny sometimes. I try and tell her about my problems and she busy telling me about hers. I also think she got a drinking problem. I swear I thought I smelled alcohol on her breath a couple times and she always be drinking from that dark blue water bottle and smiling. I wonder what is really in there. She thinks I don't know what's up."

"Tynisha, stop spreading rumors and get yourself on down to her office. You are stalling. I keep telling you to stay out of grown folk's business. Now get out of here and I'll see you tomorrow." Secretary Carrington was stern with Tynisha, yet her voice conveyed her caring posture. "Okay, Okay, I'm going. I'll see you later. Will you tell Principal Jackson I was up here looking for him?"

"I sure will and I know he'll be pleased to learn that you are following directions today and have gone almost half the day without cussing somebody out. We haven't even had to call your worker."

"Fuck child services and fuck that group home they put me at. I don't give a shit about them. Let them come, I don't care."

"Tynisha, watch your language and get on out of here. You should be careful about how you talk about the Department of Child Services. They are only trying to help you, but you keep giving them fits."

"Bye, Ms. Carrington, I don't want to talk about dem mothafuckers. I'm the one that got the shit choked out of me and I wind up getting taken out. What the hell is that? My mother didn't get arrested and she still running around the house, smacking the shit out my brothers. I don't see child services doing nothing about that shit."

"Tynisha, please."

Esther Carrington was the school secretary at Montebello for thirty years. She endured five different principals and countless assistant principals. She was familiar with many faces in the school district and always had a funny story or two to share. She raised her son in the school system, scraped to pay bills and provide him with small luxuries such as new shoes and clothing at the beginning of the school year and at Christmas. She worked hard and managed to get him accepted to the prestigious Rock Public Charter School on the outskirts of town. She vividly remembered the night she and her son, Donte, attended the lottery night to see which student applications were selected. It was in the auditorium of the fine arts center at John Memorial University because the school didn't have a large space to accommodate all the families for this particular evening. Their excitement over his and the other students acceptances were memorable nights for parents who longed for a good education for their children, but couldn't afford the tuition of private schools. The good thing about the Rock School was that over ninety percent of their students went on to attend college on full scholarship.

Peyton enjoyed a busy day of meeting with students, phoning parents, doing research on grief and loss on the computer and catching up on some outstanding paperwork, which was always too much to keep up with on a consistent basis. She always counted on a phone call from someone at the district auditing office if the paperwork wasn't completed, but she could not recall one time when she received a phone call from the auditing office asking about the well-being of any of her students. Her fellow social work colleagues said the same.

It was First Quarter Report Card Day at Montebello, dreaded by some students, and celebrated by others. Students were to report to their homeroom teacher twenty minutes before the bell rang for dismissal to receive what was known as "doom or gloom."

Peyton picked up her cell phone to send Hamilton a text message to say hello when there was a knock at her door.

"Come in."

It was Isaiah Young. "Hey, Ms. Stanfield. I was just popping in to say hello. You busy?"

Peyton set her phone down, rose from her desk, and motioned for Isaiah to come in and sit.

"No, it's okay. I was planning to pull you up probably tomorrow. I have a special opportunity for you that I think may interest you. What's up with you? How's your day going?"

"It's going good. What's the opportunity?"

"You remember the first day of school when I was walking in the hallway with a visitor?"

Isaiah gave Peyton a puzzled look.

"I think so."

"Well I was meeting with Mr. Hamilton Banks who has several businesses here in town and he is interested in mentoring a few male students here at Montebello and you were one of the students I thought of."

Isaiah looked genuinely interested. "Really? What does he want to do with us?"

"Now, that I'm not totally sure about. I think we will meet sometime in the next week to discuss specifically what he has in mind. So, are you interested?"

"Sure, Ms. Stanfield. I'll meet him. Now, I remember him. He was that good-looking, tall dude that was walking with you.

Had on a suit. Yeah, I remember now. I thought he might be a cop or something. I think he might like you, Ms. Stanfield. I saw how close he was walking to you."

Peyton tried not to look any different from her previous expression. The last thing she wanted was to give one of her students or any of the students in the building any reason to start talking about her love life. She saw that go terribly wrong with some of her colleagues. They started getting loose with their mouths, talked about their personal lives with students around and the next thing; it was all over the school this person dated that person. She knew all too well that some folks who worked in schools didn't seem to have a problem with the students knowing their personal business. That was not her. She understood to keep personal business completely separate from the students and most of her colleagues.

She ignored Isaiah's comment.

"What I will do is introduce you to him the next time he is in the building."

"Okay, Ms. Stanfield. That's cool with me. Thanks."

Peyton changed the subject. "So, tell me about this past summer. I heard you lost one of your friends from a dirt bike accident?"

Isaiah's expression suddenly turned sad.

"Yeah, my boy, Jump. We called him Jump because he always liked to jump over things, even when we were little kids. He was always jumping over something. I told him when he got that dirt bike that it might not be a good idea because he was probably gonna try and jump over something he shouldn't and that's just what happened. He tried to jump over some trashcans in the street, lost control, fell, and hit his head on the concrete curb. He got taken to the hospital, but they say he didn't make it, that he died in the ambulance."

"I'm sorry about that Isaiah. I really am."

"It's okay. I mean, I'm sad about it and I still think about him every day, but I realize that he died doing something he was probably gonna always do, so I accept it. What else can I do?"

"Okay, I hear you. That's an interesting way to get to acceptance."

"Yeah, I guess. Plus, I got other stuff on my mind now."

His expression changed to excitement.

"I met this girl, Ms. Stanfield, and she's real cute."

"Oh really? Would you like to tell me about her? Who is this girl that has you grinning from ear to ear?"

"Well, I don't know much about her yet. I met her a month ago at the flea market."

"The Franklin Flea Market?"

"No, down at Patapsco. She was with some girlfriends and came up to the same booth I was at. I say she was pretending to look at some bags so she could check me out." Isaiah had a smug look on his face.

"Okay and then what happened?"

"We started talking about the bags and ended up exchanging numbers and we been talking every day since. I've seen her two times. She lives over southeast. I think I might ask her to prom next year."

Peyton tilted her head and giggled.

"Okay, well, that's what I call thinking ahead since the prom is about a good seven months away."

Isaiah giggled back. "That's what she said when I mentioned it to her. You girls think alike."

Peyton didn't have a response and allowed him to continue to talk.

"She got a crazy family situation, Ms. Stanfield."

"Really? What's crazy about it?"

"Well, she and her older sister and her mom and dad moved here from Chicago because her mom got a job at Loyola. I think she said she was eight years old. About a year after they moved here, her parents split up and got a divorce. She says that all she remembers is that one day they stopped talking to each other and haven't really talked to each other since. She says they hate each other. She also says it makes her really sad because she's not sure if she should hate either one of them or both of them. She seems to be closest to her moms. She said her dad is mean, always busy working or dating someone new. I don't know, Ms. Stanfield. She's a nice girl, but she seems to be sad a lot."

Peyton's interest piqued. She always paid attention when discussing the topic of a sad adolescent. She remembered the year when one of her co-worker's students went home and hung herself in the basement of her parents' house. She told her friends that she was tired of being sad, but none of them thought much of it, at least, not enough to tell anyone in the school. Apparently, on the day of her demise, she made comments about being tired of all the bullshit and she would see her friends in the next life. That was a devastating time for the school, the students, and the staff. Peyton and her colleagues ended up doing a full day of training on suicide prevention for teenagers at that school.

"Have you asked what she does when feeling sad?"

"Yeah, I have. She just says that she sits in her room and listens to music. Her parents don't seem to pay a lot of attention to her because she and I are on the phone all hours of the night and nobody says anything to her. It doesn't matter whose house she's at."

"I'm sorry to hear this Isaiah because I can tell you like her and want to help her. Is there anything you think I can do?"

"No, not really. I'm just gonna talk to her some more."

"Okay, but if that changes you let me know. Also, if you feel she might really hurt herself, please call an adult or even the police if you have to. You can tell her that there are hotlines for teenagers to call if they are feeling sad or wanting to hurt themselves or someone else. If you feel comfortable doing so, you can ask her if she has talked to a counselor about her feelings, maybe somebody at her school or church, if she attends one."

"That's why I like talking to you, Ms. Stanfield. You always give me good direction."

"Thanks, Isaiah, that's good to know. It really bothers me when I hear about kids who are sad, especially because of something not going right in their family. I think all kids should be happy. There will be plenty of times in their adult life to be sad."

Isaiah nodded in agreement. Peyton couldn't understand some parents who she believed were selfish, not really giving a damn about their children. How could one think that if they didn't get along with their child's other parent that it wouldn't significantly affect their child's emotional health and well-being? Some parents didn't speak to one another and when they did, it was because they were embroiled in a bad argument. They communicated through their children exposing them to chaos and confusion.

When will parents wake up and understand that their kid's troubles are a direct reflection of their behavior? Not finding a way to communicate effectively teaches their kids to be manipulative and learn to play one parent against the other. It just makes absolutely no sense at all to me. The saying one can't choose their parents has layers and layers of meaning.

The sound of the bell signaling the students to move to their homeroom class rang and Isaiah stood up.

"Okay, Ms. Stanfield, I gotta go get my report card. Thanks for listening and I'll see you tomorrow."

"Okay, Isaiah. I hope your report card is good. Those colleges are waiting. Be safe getting home and have a good evening."

"I will Ms. Stanfield and yes I know those colleges are waiting."

He left the room, leaving Peyton thinking more about what he shared with her. She hoped this girl's parents got themselves together and began co-parenting in a manner that was beneficial to their daughter before it was too late. Consumed by the conversation, she forgot to send the hello text message to Hamilton.

Chapter Thirteen

I t was a crisp November morning as Peyton drove to work, the Thanksgiving holiday a mere week away. She thought of her plan to visit her mother and brothers at Mommy Jacqueline's home on the shore. She also thought of the crazy bunch of teachers who decided to fry a turkey on the roof of the building and nearly set the building on fire. Principal Jackson was furious. He sent an email prohibiting such behavior in the future and threatened disciplinary action. It was never a dull moment at Montebello High School.

Thinking about her day ahead, she realized she forgot about a reinstatement meeting scheduled at the last minute the previous day. It was for one of her more troubled students, Daniel, who was removed from the attendance roster at the school in what Peyton considered a questionable manner. He was an alternative education student and those students had plenty of legal rights when it came to their school life. Whatever was written into their SAP had to be executed by the school. If not, the student was entitled to compensatory awards. In Charm Town, compensatory awards ranged from cash money to computers to television sets. Daniel suddenly left late in the last school year. Principal Jackson, teachers, and students had enough of his walking the halls, calling everyone he encountered bitches and whores, and telling everybody "go fuck yourself." He refused to go to his classes and spent most of his time walking in and disrupting other classes. He threatened physical aggression to other students in the school on a daily basis. This was his third year at Montebello, but he only had enough credits earned for ninth grade status.

One day, unexpectedly, Peyton received an email that Daniel was removed from the attendance roster. She knew the removal wouldn't hold, but like everyone else in the building who tired of Daniel's antics, she was grateful for the break from him for however long it was going to last. Somehow, Daniel's father made his way to the district office to complain about how his son was "done wrong." Peyton or no one else could get him to come to the school to discuss his son's behavior and noncompliance with his medication regimen, but he was quick to go to the district. Apparently, he brought a lawyer from the Disability Law Consortium with him. That alone was most likely what got Daniel reinstated at Montebello. Whenever parents got that place involved, it usually resulted in the family getting whatever they requested. In this case, it was the reinstatement of Daniel Adams to the attendance roster of Montebello. A reinstatement meeting was scheduled to ensure the services in place for Daniel were still applicable to his needs. Peyton was unexcited about the meeting and she was sure his father would be present, most likely with his lawyer, making unreasonable demands.

Peyton was deep in her thoughts as she drove down Interstate 92 in the usual traffic when her cell phone rang. It was Gina.

"Good Morning."

"Girl, have you seen the news?" Gina sounded super-hyped on the phone.

"No, I overslept and barely had enough time for shower, makeup, and hair. I was up late last night talking to Hamilton and writing my report for that damn Daniel's reinstatement meeting I have today. He was really stressed about some work stuff. I'm supposed to meet up with him at the condo later this evening."

"Ah, I see this romance is still strong."

There was no response from Peyton and Gina continued with her breaking news.

"Well, let me tell you, this is all over the news. The principal over at Locust High School was indicted yesterday for stealing money out of the school account. I knew something was up with that dude. I saw him at a meeting last summer and he just seemed a little too smug for me. Apparently, parents were charged for their kids to participate in a weekend music and arts program that was supposed to be free. The parents were required to pay in cash and the money was never reported. I saw the story on Fox 54 this morning. They said something like fifty thousand dollars or more might have been taken from parents over the past ten years. The principal has been placed on administrative leave. They should have fired his ass on the spot. Another sad story of someone taking advantage of poor kids and families."

Peyton was quick to respond.

"It's a shame how they do these kids in Title A schools. Nobody seems to care that they are being ripped off. If Charm Town would just create a stream of funding to support supplementary educational programs, our kids and parents wouldn't have to go through all this. They are such fucking hypocrites, always saying kids first until it's time to put up some money and then it's a hundred and one excuses as to why it can't happen. They make me sick."

Peyton was annoyed. "I got to go. Hamilton is calling me. I'll see you in the building. Are you in your office?"

"Girl, I'm about twenty minutes away. I'm going to stop at Lexington Carryout and grab a breakfast sandwich. You want something?"

"You can't stop at either Cross or Hollins Carryout's? They have the French toast I like. However, I am hungry this morning and could use a bagel with cream cheese. Yeah, bring me that. Hopefully, the mice didn't get to it overnight."

"You can be such a cynic." Gina sighed. "I'll see you shortly," she said and hung up the phone.

Hamilton hung up, too, and Peyton rang him back.

"Good morning, lover. I'm sorry I didn't click over fast enough. I was on the phone with Gina and she was taking my breakfast order."

"It's okay, darling. If you're hungry, I have something you can chew on and I already know how much you like it." He had a sarcastic tone in his voice.

"Although that sounds very tempting, I have to get to the school. I have a meeting today that I need to finish prepping for. Apparently, there has been an interruption of the services of one of my students and the parent is coming with his lawyer from the Disability Law Consortium. Everyone is scrambling around trying to cover their asses. But, if I didn't have this meeting, I would certainly be pointing my car in the direction of downtown and coming and sucking the hell out of that dick of yours."

"I like it when you talk dirty to me."

"Yeah, I bet you do. What man doesn't?"

Hamilton ignored the comment. "I just wanted to hear your voice before I went into my meeting this morning. You'll appreciate this. I'm having breakfast at the Blue Moon Cafe. Not exactly my idea of the place to have a business meeting, but my lawyer loves that spot. Always talking about how they have the best breakfast in town, especially the French toast. We'll see. Then I'm headed to see my barber. Thanks for listening to me vent last night. You know I was thinking about you after we hung up and how good your body feels next to mine and how I can't wait to feel it next to me again."

"What's your meeting about?" Peyton inquired, changing the subject. No point in talking about all that, getting all worked up and not being able to do a damn thing about it.

"I'm looking into possibly expanding Lucky. I just found out about a building location that may be available. The Harbor Restaurant on Central Street closed last week after just being open under a year. The location is perfect, lots of foot and vehicle traffic and the inside has lots of space. It would be great if I could take over the lease and open The Lucky Café II. I'm talking to my lawyer and business partners about it today."

"Wow Hamilton! That sounds exciting. I hope it all works out for you. My day consists of this meeting and then a parent meeting for one of my kids who got suspended for trashing a teacher's car after she said the teacher lied on her."

"Well, that all sounds like fun. Never an idle moment with the kids, is it? Try to have a good day. Am I still seeing you later at the condo?"

"Yes, sir, you are. I miss you and can't wait to see you."

"I can't wait to see you either darling. Don't work too hard; I need you rested for me later tonight. I'll talk to you later."

"Oh wait. You still able to come next week and meet with Isaiah and the other students?

"Absolutely. Just let me know the day and time that works."

"Okay, I will. Bye, babes." Peyton clicked off the line and turned up her radio because one of her favorite tunes by one of her favorite artists, Kem, played on the radio. She immersed herself in thoughts of seeing Hamilton later as she made her way to the school building.

�֍

"Man, I know you must got a new honey on the side 'cause I ain't seen your ass in weeks." Soldier Hawkins wasted no time getting in Hamilton's shit about not coming around the barbershop. He was Hamilton's barber since before he left for college and knew all of his deeds—good and bad.

Hamilton slid in Soldier's chair and allowed him to place the nylon cape on him.

"I know, man, it's been a busy month with the Café and all. This morning I had a meeting with my lawyer about possibly expanding Lucky." He looked at Soldier through the mirror, who peered at him with pursed lips, and tilted head.

Soldier decided to go along with Hamilton's excuse just a bit longer. He knew better, but always-enjoyed taking jabs at him since he was a kid.

"I was thinking you must be trying to be one of those *new freedom fighters* and grow your 'fro out. I'm also thinking to myself that this man is either walking around looking raggedy for no reason or got himself a new barber and it better not be that and he not have the decency to tell me." Soldier sounded serious, but smiled on the inside.

"C'mon, man, you know that would never happen. Uncle Lester would rise from the grave and come whip my ass himself. I've been doing my own cut and groom. Cut a dude some slack."

"Cut you some slack?" Soldier shook his head and looked at Hamilton in disbelief.

"Naw, man, not until you tell me her name. Who is the lovely lady this time that seems to have you all twisted and presumably unfocused?" Soldier's brow furrowed and he was now serious.

Hamilton looked back at Soldier through the mirror and smiled. He just simply knew him too well. Now almost sixty years old, Soldier met Hamilton through Uncle Lester when he was twelve years old. Uncle Lester decided that it was time for Hamilton to experience the unique goings on of the Black barbershop. He remembered seeing magazines of naked women his first trip to Soldier's shop. Later in his teen years, he recalled prostitutes soliciting some men in the barbershop. Soldier and Uncle Lester met one day when Uncle Lester avoided some unpleasant people and he ducked into Soldier's shop for cover. Instead of giving him up, Soldier allowed Uncle Lester to relax in his basement storage room. Uncle Lester was eternally grateful and they became instant friends. Soldier was always kind to Hamilton and spoke with loving words at Uncle Lester's funeral, calling him "a real good man, somebody who had flaws, but also somebody who cared about the next person." In the years since his death, whenever Hamilton visited the shop, Soldier found a way to slip in the conversation how much he missed Uncle Lester, saying, "I just miss that dude, I just miss him being here and having all the answers to all the street's problems."

"Man, I done slipped up and met this girl and fell in love with her. I wait until I'm damn near forty-four years old to go out and get myself all twisted with a woman and let me tell you she is a woman not like any of my other women."

Soldier almost dropped the clippers from his hand. "What did you say? I'm getting on in my years, so I must be hearing things."

"Oh, you got jokes today. No, you're not hearing things. I've been seeing a very special lady who just makes me happy. She's fine, funny, smart, intriguing and tons of fun. She complements me pretty good, too. Honestly, I'm shocked as hell about it 'because it all happened so fast and so unexpectedly. She walked in my restaurant one day and I was right away attracted to her. Then I see her when I go with Sandra on the first day of school to visit a school I'm planning to volunteer with. She's one of the social workers on staff there. As soon as I saw her, I'm thinking to myself, this must be fate. Me being me, I immediately turn on my charm and the minute I get alone with her, I ask her to join me for lunch at Lucky. Turns out, she was attracted to me as well."

By this time, Soldier put down the clippers and stood next to Hamilton with his hands on his hips listening to the story. Hamilton continued.

"So, she accepts my invitation to lunch and we've been seeing each other ever since. I even gave her the key to the penthouse."

Soldier looked completely stunned and eyed Hamilton with a scowl on his face. "Does Sandra know about this one?"

Hamilton answered very confidently. "No"

"Are you sure 'cause I'm not sure how much more she can take. That woman has put up with a lot from you and barely gives you shit about it. She's going straight to heaven, after she does her stint in hell."

Both men burst out in laughter. Soldier knew Sandra and her family. He continued. "Okay, so what makes this one different? I knew something was up with you. I haven't seen nor heard from you in weeks and you come in here looking unlike your usual smug, self-assured self.

"I know, Solge." Hamilton sometimes cut off pronouncing Soldier's entire name.

"I know you won't believe me, but it's really hard for me to explain. She's great and we get along great. I can talk with her and we laugh at the craziest things. She's not all uptight like Sandra can be. At first I thought it was just gonna be a few sex dates, but after about the third time hanging out with her, I realized I *really* like this woman. And, she has this innocence about her that's not so innocent. I mean it's not like she is a virgin or anything, but she is a bit inexperienced in the sex department and that turned me on more than her body, which is hot. I like being her first in a lot of things sexually."

Soldier faced Hamilton and nodded in agreement.

"You've got answers for everything, so what are you going to do?"

"Dude, I ain't got an answer for this one. I don't know. I do know I have fallen for her and you know I've never fallen for any of my women. I think about her all the time. She is just so different and I can't put my finger on exactly why. I probably should stop seeing her because things are sure to get messy, but I don't want to. I actually want her in my bed with me every night."

"How's she sexing you?"

"What? Amazingly, and she's open to whatever I ask of her. Like I said, surprisingly, I initially found her to be a little sexually naïve. She hasn't had a lot of different experiences, but she is not afraid to share her body and has no restrictions. Not a prude like Sandra and some of those other chicks I was doing. Her body is sexy as hell and she's got these dimples on her face that are just adorable. I can't get enough of her and when I'm fucking her, I want to fuck her either all day or all night."

"So what are you saying? You're in love?"

"I'm not saying love yet, but I am saying that I don't see an end in sight with her and I'm not looking for one."

"How old is she?"

"She's in her thirties."

"Married, any kids?"

"Nope to both."

"Does she want either?"

"I don't know. We haven't talked about any of that yet."

"She got a boyfriend?"

"She says no and I told her I didn't want her seeing nobody else while we are together."

"You are such the pimp. And she knows you're married?"

"Of course, you know I don't lie about that stuff."

"I don't know man. She might be thinking you could leave your family, marry her and give her at least one kid. It sounds like she's at the age where she might be thinking about that."

"That has crossed my mind and it has also crossed my mind to consider leaving Sandra. You know it's something I've thought about at least for the past five years. I haven't given it a lot of thought because I hadn't met anyone that moved me to even consider such a thing, until now."

"What about the kids? Would you leave them? I know how you feel about them."

"Now that would probably be the one thing that breaks me. I love Sandra, but our love has changed. It's more about the business now. I think we have different outlooks on our futures. She's a great mother and a good woman and I really don't want to hurt her 'because we both know, she has put up with a lot from me over the years and we've also shared a lot together. We were so young when we met, started dating, and got married."

Soldier picked up his clippers and sighed before he spoke.

"Well, my friend, I'd say you got yourself one hell of a little problem."

Hamilton had no response. He looked back at Soldier in the mirror and nodded in agreement. The problem was much bigger than Soldier would ever know.

⚘

"I love him," Peyton said simply, matter-of-factly and with a stern tone.

She and Gina sat in the teacher's lounge because Gina was having one of her sugar fits and asked Peyton to go with her when the dismissal bell rang to get a sweet bun out of the vending machine. She hoped it worked and was full with goodies. Many times, the vending machines in the teacher's lounge were empty for weeks before being refilled. The teacher's lounge was known for three things: being dirty, hardly used by the actual teachers and a storage place for broken computers, printers and other items no longer used. Oftentimes, hall monitors, teacher substitutes, and sports coaches used the lounge on a regular basis because they had no space of their own. Each year, a sign mysteriously appeared, reminding the adults to clean up after themselves, remove their food from the refrigerator before it would become unrecognizable, and not take other people's items.

Gina looked at her with a pitiful and stern face.

"Peyton, what are you talking about?"

"I'm talking about the fact that I love Hamilton and before you get started on your 'he's married' speech, I am well aware of that fact and I love him regardless. Besides, he tells me all the time he and his wife have a loveless marriage and it's based upon their kids and their business dealings. I know you don't like all this, but he and I really have an amazing energy and chemistry together. I know it hasn't been that long since we met, but the truth is I knew the moment I laid eyes on him he was something special. When it's just him and me, it feels like there is no better place on earth, pure joy from beginning to end. It's all about me, barely any distractions and I never want to leave him. I've already told you that the sex is unbelievable, at least for me. I think I may be a little too slow for him though. Oh, and before you ask, he told me he's not seeing anyone else but me."

Gina couldn't recall another time when Peyton sounded so naïve, like some innocent little school girl, but she decided it was pointless to lecture her about allowing herself to first, become involved with a married man and second, to actually fall in love with his ass.

Who does that? Only those who actually do fall in love.

She decided she would be sympathetic with her friend.

"Okay, so, why are you telling me this and what are you going to do?"

Peyton paused before answering. "That's a good question and you know I don't really have an answer. I guess I just need to talk to someone about my feelings for Hamilton, someone who won't judge me or make me feel like shit. It's not as if I can really talk with anyone else about this situation, definitely not my mother. I'm not going to do anything right now, just enjoy every time I get to see him."

"You *really* do love him." Gina sounded genuinely surprised. She never imagined her friend would allow herself to develop feelings for the situation.

"Yeah, I do. Do I sound stupid?" Peyton stared at her, looking for an honest answer.

Gina was honest, too. "No, you don't sound stupid. You just sound like a woman who is in love. You had no idea this was going to happen and so goddamned fast. It's not as if you set out to meet a married man and fall head over heels for him. You can't help but love him. He's amazing. I knew it was over for you from the beginning when you came to the car back in August, panting and raving about how he was so good-looking. When I went back and asked Walter about him, he didn't really have anything real bad to say about him. But, I have to tell you what you already know.

"What's that?"

"Love can be a funny thing, makes people do all sorts of things they wouldn't ordinarily do." Gina nudged Peyton on the arm with her shoulder.

Grateful that her best girlfriend lightened the conversation, Peyton smiled at her and giggled. "Am I that bad and that obvious?"

Gina tilted her head to the side, looking at her with wide eyes. She didn't have to say a word.

Peyton giggled again. "Okay, okay, I get it."

Chapter Fourteen

"Where do you want to go to dinner?" Peyton preferred Hamilton select the restaurant because he had great taste for food.

"Hmm, I was thinking maybe we could check out Kali's Court down in Covington Square. Have you been?"

"No, but some of the teachers at the school have talked about it, saying it's a little pricey, but very good. Last year, some of the students chose that place as the dinner spot for the Valentine's Day dance."

"Okay, well since you don't have to worry about prices, Kali's Court it is. I'll make us a reservation for seven."

"Are we staying at the condo tonight?"

"Yes, darling, we are. Is there a problem with that?"

"Nope, no problem here, I'm looking forward to it. I just need to pack my bag for work tomorrow, although because the students will be testing, I can go in late. I'll have some time to do you a little longer tonight and tomorrow morning. I love waking up next to you with that incredible view of downtown."

"Now that sounds like a perfect plan to me. Okay, I'll meet you here and then we can drive over together. Oh, and if we weren't on the phone, I'd take you up on your do me a little longer offer *right now.*"

"Hahahaha, you're funny. Sounds good. I'll see you later, and Hamilton…. I miss you."

"I miss you, too, darling. I'll be looking at the clock every hour until it's time for you to get here."

❧

Kali's Court was on the list of Charm Town's favorite restaurants for years. It was an enjoyable place, with amazing food and spectacular service. Hamilton enjoyed driving up in his Audi sports coupe, jumping out and waving to all the parking attendants who were familiar with him. Inside, they sat in one of the private rooms located in the back of the restaurant. Hamilton said it would allow them the opportunity to really talk and enjoy one another, but she also knew it was also not to be seen by someone who knew either one of them and their personal situations.

Dinner with Hamilton was always an experience: wine selections, soups and salads, appetizers, main courses, dessert, and after dinner cocktails. He liked to experience all that a restaurant offered. Peyton assumed it had to do with the fact he was a restaurant owner and was always around food. Kali's was a great atmosphere and after her second French Martini, she felt very comfortable and confident.

"So, Mr. Hamilton, what is it about me that has you so enticed? From where I sit, you just can't seem to get enough of me."

He looked unsurprised and unfazed. "You really want to know?"

Suddenly, she got nervous.

Oh shit, what's he going to say?

"Yeah, I really want to know and if you want to know, I'll tell you."

"Okay, that's fine, but before we get into all that, tell me about your day. What new adventures occurred at my favorite school today?"

"It was a good day, not too much happened. A lot of kids were out. The school tends to experience a drop in attendance right after the Thanksgiving break and before the Christmas break. Some of the kids think they can start their vacation early and some just don't want to adjust to the change in temperature. They aren't used to the cold, yet. I was able to catch up on some of my notes but I did get a little upset today."

Hamilton looked interested. "Oh, yeah? What happened?"

"It's really stupid. I had gone to the SAP office to make some copies and Ms. Chadwick was trying to get on me for using the paper to make copies. She acts as if she bought that damn paper herself. That's what has gotten on my nerves about this system. They always expect the teachers and support staff to go above and beyond for the kids, which most of us don't mind doing, but then barely give you enough funds to buy paper. Paper! I'm not talking about brand new Apple computers for each kid. I'm talking about *paper*. Every school I've been to, somebody has made a big deal out of paper. You would think that stuff was laced in gold or something. And, let's not even start talking about how hard it is to get soap, toilet paper, and paper towels put in the bathrooms. Those are just luxuries you can't always get in Charm Town schools. She just really got on my nerves, that's all."

Hamilton looked perplexed. She was sure this was all news to him.

"Wow, I'm sorry to hear that and it all sounds really childish to me. I never had that problem at Gilman."

"It is and that's my point. It's always something going on in that building. Oh, there is this new rumor going around about the new economics teacher. The story is he has a side job as a stripper up in New York on the weekends. I don't know if it's true, but folks are talking about it. Apparently, a student overheard his conversation with someone on the phone talking about he didn't get paid his proper money over the weekend and he don't take his clothes off for free." Peyton laughed.

"Oh, and you find that funny?"

She continued to laugh. "I sure do. I'm trying to imagine, throwing your clothes off for horny women on Sunday, and standing in front of a bunch of horny teenagers presenting a lesson on Monday."

Hamilton smiled and got back to the original subject.

"My time with you has been of the upmost of pleasure for me. I have not met anyone quite like you in a long time, Ms. Peyton Stanfield. You want to know what entices me about you? Well, the answer would be everything. I'm enticed by your free spirit, your passion for what you do, your willingness to try new things, your drive, your view of the world, your interest in me and obviously, your looks and your body, but I think you may already know that."

Peyton blushed and continued to listen to Hamilton who looked very serious.

"I'm glad I have you all to myself. I know it's selfish of me to request and require this but I think I have done a pretty good job of showing you that I don't intend to play games with you or your heart. I don't know where this is going and I can't promise you anything now, except that I will never disrespect you and I will do my best to make you feel very special all the times you are with me."

Peyton stared at Hamilton in disbelief at what she heard. She liked what he said, but felt like she was the main character in some fairytale book, and this was not really happening.

"Sandra is my wife and I don't have plans to divorce her and I need for you to be okay with that. I'll repeat that we do not live as a married couple. We haven't made love for over five years and we sleep in separate rooms when I stay at the house. We purchased the downtown condo with the understanding that I would be staying there a lot. As I shared with you before, she has agreed to not come there unless under special circumstances of which I would be aware. That is why I felt comfortable gifting you a key. She will never show up there and I want you to feel free to be in my presence as much as you desire and I hope that's all the time."

Hamilton noticed the puzzled look on Peyton's face. He reached out, grabbed her hand, and rubbed it gently.

"Darling, are you okay?"

Peyton smiled, as she rubbed his hand.

"Yeah, I'm okay; I just don't know what to say. I've wanted to hear this from you. I, I have absolutely loved the time we have spent together and I don't want it to end. I don't care that you are married and I believe what you have said about your relationship with Sandra. I just want to be with you. No one has made me feel the way you do and I just don't want to give up the feeling I get when I'm with you. Just so you know, I'm not seeing anyone else. I know I told you before but I want to make sure you understand that I've never been one who could sleep with two men at the same time. No disrespect to the gals who do, I just can't do that and I don't want to with you. I get attention from guys, single guys, and I'm not interested in any of them. I keep thinking about you, Hamilton. I think about you all the time.

I've thought of you every day since we met. I practically talk Gina's ear off about you."

Hamilton smiled. "You warm my heart, darling, you warm my heart."

At that moment, Peyton stood up and planted a kiss on Hamilton's forehead. "And you warm more than my heart. I'm not going anywhere. I love being with you and I'm not afraid to say it. I'm also not afraid to say that I've fallen in love with you."

Hamilton stood up and embraced Peyton in his signature hug. "Thank you, darling. Trust me; you will not regret anything. Just allow me to take care of you and I'm surely falling in love with you."

Peyton held on to the hug, squeezing him tightly. It was exactly what she wanted to hear.

"I like a little pain." Hamilton looked straight up at the ceiling while lying nude on the bed, his left leg intertwined with Peyton's. Lying naked on her side, she propped her head up with her right arm, and stared at him in part disbelief, part shock and part excitement.

It just gets better and better with him, she thought.

The room was dark with the exception of the light illuminating from the BOSE stereo system on the entertainment center in front of the bed and the streaks of light sneaking between the shears at the window. It was a full moon outside and the light streaked across Hamilton's bare chest.

Pain? Peyton continued to watch him looking at the ceiling with a focused stare and wondered what he meant by his statement. After a brief silence, she asked him.

"What kind of pain?"

He doesn't know it, but I'll do whatever he wants raced through her mind. She saw some of the sex shows where the girl or guy was tied up and all kinds of other sado-masochistic-type stuff. It was foreign to her, but for Hamilton, she would try almost anything.

"Biting. I like my woman to bite me on my neck and chest and dig her nails in my back. It's an amazing turn on." Hamilton spoke in his soft, sensual tone, eyes still fixated on the ceiling.

"Uh, well, I don't know if I could inflict pain on you." Peyton said in a low, hesitant tone.

He untangled his leg from hers, turned gently toward her, and stared directly into her eyes. With his dark and mysterious eyes, she swore he looked deep into her soul.

"Darling, I'm not asking you to do something you aren't comfortable doing. What I am asking is that you allow me to bring your body to total submission, complete surrender. I don't think you have ever been to that place before, have you?"

OMG! Peyton was embarrassed, swallowed hard, and grateful the light was not shining on her face. She knew Hamilton was aware of her minimal sexual adventures and she felt he somehow took delight in that information. It was uncomfortable for her because she always seemed to be in a learning curve with him, especially when it came to sex. She loved and trusted him and knew he wouldn't intentionally do something to hurt her.

Suddenly, he slid his lean body off the satin sheets, off the bed, and stood up over her.

"Come with me. Let's go downstairs. I want to get something to eat."

Eat? We, not too long ago, had a six-course dinner.

Like an obedient child, she got off the bed and slipped on the rouge-colored, button-down, dress shirt that he loved for her to wear when she wore nothing else. He wasn't one of those guys who wanted his woman in skimpy lingerie, thongs, or sexy costumes. The simple button down dress shirt did it for him.

He slipped on a pair of Nike shorts, took Peyton's hand, and led her out the roomy bedroom and toward the stairway. Halfway down the stairs, he abruptly stopped and turned to face her. Without saying a word, he cupped her face with his large, smooth hands and began to kiss her, first her forehead, then her eyes, then her nose, then her cheeks, her ears and finally her mouth. His kisses consumed her entire mouth. They were wet, passionate, and long. He liked to feel all of Peyton's tongue in his mouth and he liked to put all of his tongue in her mouth.

Just as she got lost in his kiss, he moved to her neck and kissed both sides. Peyton felt his arms move around her waist and suddenly her body was in his arms and he was lowering her to the stair, placing her down, and spreading her legs open, revealing no panties, just the shirt. His silhouette in the darkness was alluring. He began to smile.

"Shhh, don't talk," he whispered, as he lowered his head between her thighs. She lifted her legs, positioning one on the wall and the other on the railing, leaned back on the stairway and let out a slow, low moan. Hamilton Banks gave the best oral sex she ever experienced. His tongue explored every part of her clitoris and vagina, slowly and methodically. He moved his soft hands, cupping her buttocks and licking her inner thighs, and up and down her legs. She was happy she shaved the night before as she looked down and began to stroke his head as he stroked her with his tongue.

"Ohhhhh," she moaned deeply. "Hamilton, oh my God, shit, this feels so good."

"Shhh, you have to be quiet," he whispered and then went back to work. "Don't move, darling. I want to bring your body to

214 | *Hunter William*

total surrender. I want you to surrender completely to me right here, right now."

Peyton barely maintained herself and placed her hand over her mouth to keep from letting out the loudest shrieks of pleasure. Her body moved in unison with Hamilton's mouth, as his tongue continued to explore her. She closed her eyes and rolled her head back, touching the stair.

"Oh, oh, *ohhhhh*," Peyton shrieked, as she grabbed his head with her left hand and grabbed the stair railing with her right. She positioned herself for the big orgasm she felt coming on at lightning speed.

"*Ahhhhh!*" she shrieked, as she lifted her body up as she came in a moment of explosion. Her body twitched several times after as she lay limp, legs still open on the stairway.

Hamilton lifted his head. "I'm not done yet. I want total surrender. Stand up," he ordered.

"But Hamilton, my legs," Peyton began to say. Before she could say more, he put his hand over her mouth.

"Shhh, remember, don't talk. You trust me, right? Now stand up and turn around. I want to enter this beautiful ass from behind."

She could barely move, but she was a docile girl when it came to him. She lifted her body up and turned around. He bent her over and lifted up the shirt, again exposing her behind.

"Bend your knees," he said, as she felt him enter her. It was quick and smooth even though she was tight. "Oh, you are nice and tight for Daddy," he whispered in her ear. "And, I like the way you are giving it to me. It's like you *really, really* want me to have it."

He began to stroke her slowly and then with long, quick thrusts. He made it clear in previous sexual encounters that he didn't care how sore she became. "It's part of the process of total submission. You can always get iced if you need to," was all he said to her when she complained about the soreness, which sometimes lasted two or more days.

"That's a good girl. Now I want you to come for me."

Peyton's body was on fire. She knew she no longer was in control of her bodily functions, rhythms, or movements. Hamilton Banks had stamina and he could stay in her for hours. After what seemed an endless period of his strokes in and out of her, she let out a loud shriek and came all over him.

"Good, girl…good, girl. That's what I want and you are *so* wet."

Peyton slumped back in his arms, exhausted and exhilarated. His powerful arms were able to catch her with ease.

He stroked her a few more times before he gently pulled out of her. She slouched as she turned and slumped on the steps. Her vagina was pulsating and felt raw. He picked her up, carried her over to the chaise lounge in the entertainment room, placed her down gently, and stretched her body the length of the chair. He retrieved the fleece blanket draped over the chair and covered her with it. Bending down on one knee, he looked down at her smiling up at him.

"Wait here, I'll get you some water," he said, as he stood up and walked toward the kitchen. She stared at his shirtless body as he walked away from her. She naïvely imagined she could live like this with him forever.

"I thought we came down so you could get something to eat," she managed to whisper before drifting off to sleep.

"I just ate," were the last words she heard him say.

Chapter Fifteen

The Montebello High School Annual staff holiday party was in full swing when Peyton and Gina walked down from Peyton's office. They had prepared the Secret Santa baskets for those that dared to participate. It was always a humorous activity as most of the names exchanged were between teachers and staff who had secret crushes on each other. While arranging the packages, Peyton and Gina speculated who would end up as the night hookups. Gina revealed her picks first.

"You know, Ms. Darden picked Mr. Branson."

"You mean Mr. Branson, the cute, new hall monitor?"

"Yep, that's the one. Scandalous, right?"

"It sure is. What is she, about forty and what is he, about twenty-five?"

Gina laughed at Peyton. "No, you know he's not that young. I think he's like twenty-nine, thirty years old."

"Damn, she's trying to get her groove back, isn't she?"

"Actually, no not really. I've worked with her before and she's known to date younger men. I remember her telling me her first husband was about ten years younger than her."

"Hey, if it works, then who am I to hate on her? She got her thing and I got mine. She's loving her thing and I'm damn sure loving mine."

Gina rolled her eyes at Peyton. "Am I going to hear about the fabulous Hamilton Banks again, for the tenth time today?"

"Shut up, I'm not saying nothing more about Hamilton 'because it's obvious you don't want to hear anything more."

"*Whatever!* Stop getting all serious on me. You know I'm just kidding. You can talk about his fine ass as much as you want with me 'cause I'm sure I'm the only one that will listen to you."

Peyton laughed. "I think you are right about that mainly because you are the only one that knows about him."

"Did you spend last night with him?"

"Yeah, he made me dinner and then he fucked me half the night."

"And are you complaining?"

"Absolutely not."

"You are such a tramp."

"And you are so jealous."

Gina nodded. "That might be true 'because I've been dry lately. I don't know what's going on, but no one's calling me. I've had to go home every night and look at Bert's face."

"You sound as if that is such a bad thing."

"It's not. He's just boring as hell."

"Shut up, Gina. That man loves you and would do just about anything for you."

Gina shrugged. "Yeah, he does. I can't deny that."

"Thank goodness you are finally giving him some good credit."

Gina was ready to respond when Principal Jackson's voice came over her walkie-talkie.

"Ms. Carey, come in please."

Gina looked to the ceiling and took a deep breath. "Go ahead, Principal Jackson."

There was inaudible noise in the background mixed with his muffled voice.

"Can you come outside to the corner of Baker Street? I'm out here with Officer Barnett and one of the drivers of the Metro bus. Apparently, several of our students and some students from Harbor High School got into a fight on the bus and broke several windows. He needs help completing his report and I have to get to the auditorium for the debate team's practice. They head to Harvard tomorrow for the national championships."

"Okay, I'm on my way out there now." Gina stood up. "I got to go. Sometimes these kids get on my nerves. Fighting on the damn bus? That's why we keep getting calls from the neighbors about some of the kids being rude and disrespectful on the bus. It's getting so bad that the elderly residents avoid taking the bus early in the morning when they're coming to school and for at least an hour after dismissal time. Then people want to wonder why there are some calls to cease using the public transit service as the means for transporting the kids to and from school."

Peyton saw Gina's frustration on her face. "Today is one of those days I'm glad I'm not an administrator. Go and do your job, Ms. Vice Principal, and I'll see you at the party."

"Oh, so you are going to come? I just knew you were going to tell me you were going down to the condo."

"No, not yet. I'm going to hang out here for a bit, but I will be seeing him later."

Gina flashed Peyton the thumbs up. "Cool, I'll see you after I take care of this latest fiasco. Actually, I'll come back up here and we can go down together."

"Okay, that works for me."

Each year, Principal Jackson held the party a few weeks before the Christmas holiday. Most of the teachers dressed in fancy, holiday attire and were in great moods. It was a potluck affair, with each staff person making a dish or contributing money toward the purchase of food. It was always funny to see whose dish was the first and last to be eaten. That determination was based upon the perception of a person's cleanliness. If they appeared dirty, everyone made excuses not to eat the dish. If a person appeared clean, their dish was one of the first to go. Principal Jackson, back from the debate team's practice, handed out his gifts to the staff.

"Ho, ho, ho, and Merry Christmas." He wore a Santa hat atop his baldhead and was in a festive mood. "To all those who have been naughty *and* nice."

Gina and Peyton sat at a round table with Ms. Edna, the custodian, and the teachers from the math department. Ms. Edna couldn't resist commenting.

"Look at Jackson over there. He looks like he's been in that Crown Royal again."

Everyone at the table eyed her with a surprised expression and Peyton spoke first.

"Ms. Edna, what are you talking about? You know Principal Jackson is just being festive 'because it's a *festive* time."

"Yeah, okay. Festive my ass. He looks drunk to me and that ain't the first time."

The teachers at the table continued to look shocked.

Ms. Edna is acting as if she's had a few Crown Royals herself.

Peyton changed the subject.

"Ms. Edna, you are funny. What you got going on for Christmas break?"

"Nothing. I'm just gonna stay around my house and clean up. I usually do a Christmas Eve dessert party, but that's about it."

Peyton was grateful she didn't challenge her for changing the subject.

"Oh okay, that sounds like fun."

"It is. I get my girlfriends to come over and we play Christmas carols and each of us makes a different dessert and of course, we have our spirits. By the end of the night, we all are drunk. I barely make it to church services the next morning."

Just then, the music began playing. Principal Jackson used his BOSE speaker system and his iPod to blast The Temptations, and it was extra fun after a few cups of the spiked eggnog.

The party was several hours of dancing, laughs, and good conversation among some of the staff. Peyton and Gina mingled among the teachers and remained until the end. Principal Jackson approached them once all the teachers exited the room.

"You ladies enjoyed yourselves tonight?"

Both nodded and Peyton spoke first. "We sure did and thanks for the gifts."

"No problem, it's my pleasure. Just a little something to show my appreciation for everyone's hard work. So, whose food wasn't eaten tonight? I wasn't hungry so I didn't go over to the table."

Gina looked surprised. "What? You didn't eat? Now that's a first."

"What are you trying to say, Ms. Carey, that I like to eat a lot?"

Gina smirked. "Well, if the shoe fits."

Peyton took a step back and let them go at each other.

"I don't think I appreciate your tone of voice," Principal Jackson snapped.

"What you mean? I just asked a question. You are way too sensitive, Jackson."

"And you are way too smart." He winked at her.

"I got to get going. I have the district administrator's holiday party tomorrow down at the Woodberry Kitchen. I hear this year the school board members will be attending, including the president, Sandra Banks. I have no idea what that's about."

Peyton and Gina looked at Principal Jackson with blank stares.

"What? Why are you two looking crazed?"

Gina spoke first. "What do you mean? We're just surprised you're planning to go, considering you are so anti-school board."

He had no idea of the real reason.

"Yeah, I'm going to go. Might as well see what's going on because whenever board members tag along, something is going on and I'd rather be on the front end of bad news as opposed to the back end."

Neither Gina nor Peyton said anything. They simply raised their eyebrows and nodded in agreement.

✤

"Girl, I almost choked when Jackson mentioned Sandra's name." Peyton phoned Gina on her way to Hamilton's condo.

"I know and I didn't know how to respond, which is why I kept my mouth shut."

"I wonder what she wants with them."

"Ain't no telling with that bunch. One thing is for sure, that's one time you can rendezvous with her husband and not worry about her showing up and ruining the party."

"Shut up, Gina. You are not funny."

"I'm not trying to be."

Chapter Sixteen

The intensity of her feelings for Hamilton consumed and frightened Peyton. Convincing herself she needed space, she abruptly, without conversation, distanced herself from him for two weeks. She didn't call him and refused to answer his calls, text messages, or emails. She felt agonized and tortured. She spent a majority of the time thinking of him and she missed him with a surprising fervor. Listening to Gina, she thought it was good to put some space between them to sort her feelings and gain better perspective. She felt bad she acted selfishly and immature and hadn't communicated her fearful feelings to him. Thankfully, he was mostly out of town in New York City on business because she was sure he would have come to the school looking for her. Besides, she was busy attending to the needs of her students during this time after the first marking period and before Christmas break.

She sat at a red light on The Alameda as she read and responded to his latest text message.

Hamilton: Is today the day you will speak with me again?

Peyton: Today is the day. I'm so sorry. I'm scared of my intense feelings for you. I thought if I just put some space between us, my feelings would cool off.

Hamilton: So, have they cooled off?

Peyton: No, they are stronger. All I've done is tortured myself.

Hamilton: Don't be scared, my darling. Mine are stronger as well. I have missed you terribly and I'm disappointed you would cut me off in such a manner. Please promise me you will not do that again without talking with me first. We are in this together. You don't have to feel this way alone.

Peyton: I don't know what I was thinking. Again, I'm sorry.

Hamilton: All is forgiven, but you will have to let me stroke you a bit longer when I finally get back inside you.

Peyton: I suppose I can handle that.

Hamilton: Good because I've been holding out and can't be responsible for how I leave your kitty cat.

Peyton: I guess I deserve that comment.

Hamilton: Don't fret, my sunshine, I'm just happy you're okay. I was thinking either something happened to you or you finally met Prince Charming and decided to dump my ass.

Peyton: I've already met Prince Charming.

Hamilton: And he is happy to know you. Now that all this nonsense is behind us, will I see you later at the condo?

Peyton: Yes.

⁂

Later that day, Peyton showered, dressed, and headed down to the Presidential. She missed Hamilton and couldn't wait to see him. Mr. Edgar seemed happy to see her.

"Good evening, Ms. Peyton. It's so nice to see you. I've not seen you recently; I suppose we have been missing each other?"

"No, Mr. Edgar, you haven't been missing me. This is my first time here in a c couple weeks."

Mr. Edgar gave Peyton a look of concern. He knew Hamilton was married to Sandra.

"Well, Ms. Peyton, if you are happy then I'm happy for you. You seem like a nice person and I wouldn't want to see you get hurt."

Peyton knew what he was referring to, but chose to ignore the comment.

"It's good to see you, Mr. Edgar. I'll be heading up now. Would you mind buzzing Hamilton and letting him know that I am on my way up?"

Mr. Edgar turned up his mouth and nodded. "Sure, Ms. Peyton. It will be my pleasure."

She watched him dial Hamilton, as the elevator doors closed. For a second she wondered what he thought. "I don't care what he thinks," she mumbled to herself.

The elevator doors opened and Hamilton stood with a relieved expression, arms outstretched and held a single lavender lily.

Look at him. All I've accomplished from this silly hiatus of mine was to torture myself because I just want to be with him. Time away has not changed that.

"Well hello there darling. Aren't you a welcome sight? Come here and give me a hug. I have missed you."

Peyton stepped off the elevator and rushed into Hamilton's arms, practically smashing the lily he held. Without a word, she planted a kiss on him that she wanted to continue forever.

He returned the kiss with his usual passion and intensity that always made her want to succumb to his advances forever. Before too long he pulled away.

"Hey, wait a minute. I got this for you." He handed her the lily. I saw it this afternoon when I was walking around at Belvedere Shops and instantly thought of your pretty face. Are you hungry?" His body language and tone of voice communicated him wanting nothing else, but to see her.

At that moment, she realized the place smelled the aroma of something good.

"What is that amazing smell?"

"My creation for you, my lady. Why don't you get settled wherever you would like and then we can eat. I have some wine chilling on the kitchen counter and I've taken the liberty to pour you a glass. It's over there waiting for you."

Peyton forgot all about needing to take a break to get control of her feelings. That was a joke anyway, as she was already in too deep.

"Thanks. I'm so sorry..."

"Shh, let's not speak about that, especially since I'm confident it won't be happening again."

Peyton's eyes watered. "No, it won't."

"Good because I don't like my girl acting like she's not my girl. You were about to tell me something."

"Yeah, just that it's been a crazy week at that school and some of those kids really need to be in another place. They disrupt the entire classroom environment. Poor Ms. Burroughs is disrespected every day. Just because she is an older teacher, the kids in her class think they can treat her any way they choose. It's awful and I hate to see it, but what can I do? I'm not the principal or part of the discipline team."

Hamilton grabbed Peyton's hands and began softly massaging them. "Darling, I just got you back so please don't get yourself too stressed. Tonight I don't want to hear about Montebello, I just want to hear about you."

"I know. I just hate to see anyone being mistreated, especially by some rude, no-home-training kids."

"Listen, go grab your wine and let's just relax and soothe ourselves."

"Well that absolutely sounds like a plan to me." Another kiss was in order.

Peyton made her way to the kitchen and couldn't help looking in the pots. Everything smelled great and looked amazing. She couldn't wait to taste his latest culinary creation and then taste him.

The meal of grilled trout, braised Brussels sprouts, and cheese risotto was scrumptious. By dinner's end, she consumed two, full glasses of wine and was feeling very relaxed. She helped Hamilton clean the kitchen before they relaxed in his living room, overlooking the beautiful Charm Town harbor. It was a picturesque night and she knew she wasn't going to want it to end. Although she was staying the night, it just never seemed to be enough time with him.

"You feel like watching a movie?" Hamilton asked, as he lay on the oversized couch, caressing Peyton's breasts. "I can order something off the cable network or maybe have Edgar run out and get something, especially if there is a particular flick you want to see."

"No, you don't have to worry Mr. Edgar. I don't want to be a bother to him."

"Darling, you are no bother. Why would you say that?"

Peyton started lying. "I don't know. It just feels funny to have someone run around town getting something as silly as a movie for me."

Hamilton eyed Peyton suspiciously. He sat up on the couch, leaving her slouched and breasts exposed.

"Okay, Peyton, why don't you just tell me what is really bugging you about Edgar. You know he's a cool man and he has gotten things for me repeatedly, so tell me what's up please because you know I know when you are not being totally forthcoming. Your forehead begins to sweat and you seem to have a hard time looking directly into my eyes."

"Hamilton, I always have a hard time looking into your eyes. I'm afraid you'll see how vulnerable I really am to you."

He continued to look directly into her eyes.

"Stop bullshitting and get to the real point." He began to caress her hair. "Because if you don't, I'll have to do this to you."

At that moment, he slid down to the floor, pulling her down across the chaise part of the couch. He quickly removed the only piece of clothing she wore, her underpants, and performed his signature oral pleasure. Between tongue strokes, he would raise his head and ask, "Are you ready to tell me yet?"

Peyton, who morphed into a state of ecstasy, purposefully took a few extra minutes to give up the information.

Hell, oral sex with this man is better than most things I can think of and I'm not ready for this to stop. He's got skills.

After several more minutes of pleasure, she spoke.

"Okay, it's because I know he knows you're married and that I'm the mistress. I sometimes feel like he looks at me as if I'm his daughter and he wants to scold me when I come over. I don't know; it just feels a little weird."

Hamilton lifted his head, long enough to respond.

"Does this feel weird?" He flashed his mischievous grin, ignoring her concerns regarding Mr. Edgar.

"Absolutely not and please don't stop."

Suddenly, he got back on the chaise where she laid, body wet from the sweat, vagina soaked from his tongue and anticipation of his entrance into her.

Is this man crazy? She looked at him quizzically.

Hamilton acted as if he didn't recognize the expression.

"Darling, listen. I don't want you to worry about Edgar. Trust me when I tell you he doesn't think like that. He knows my relationship with Sandra has been dead for a long time and he's happy to see I have met someone who makes me feel alive and spontaneous and not to mention freaky." He winked, as he planted a kiss on her cheek.

"I'm sorry if I sound as if I'm a teenager, but it's how I have been feeling."

"And it stops now. I don't want you having any sort of those feelings when you come over here. I told you, Peyton, I want you here with me and that's that. Now get your pretty self on up and let's get to the bedroom. I want to finish what I started."

"No argument with that. I was thinking you just might leave me hanging and feigning for you all night."

Hamilton rose off the couch, pulling Peyton with him, giving a hug that felt eternal.

"Never, darling. I'll never leave you hanging."

Peyton and Hamilton made love for most of the night. She remembered looking at the clock that read 4:50 AM before she fell off to sleep in his arms.

The next morning, Peyton awoke to the phone ringing. She knew it was Edgar from downstairs because of the tone of the ring. She didn't answer, assuming he was looking for Hamilton and she knew he left for an early morning meeting with some business people about the Christmas season at The Lucky Café. Rolling over in the bed, she noticed another single lily and the small Smyth Jewelers box on the nightstand. He presented the Rebecca bracelet to her the night before, surprising her, saying he merely wanted to get something special for someone special. He had no problem demonstrating his affinity for her.

The phone rang again, several times, but Peyton continued to ignore Mr. Edgar. She wanted to linger in the aroma of the loved-on sheets a little longer before getting her day started. It was the last day of school before Christmas break, which meant the school was mostly empty and her timely presence was not required. Lying naked, she buried her face in the sheets, trying to inhale the scent of Hamilton's body. Last night, he made her feel special, almost as if she really were the center of his world.

She was almost off in a deep sleep when she heard the door to the bedroom open. Excited he was back with her, she abruptly sat up in the bed.

"Good morning, sweetness."

It wasn't Hamilton.

"Good morning, Ms. Stanfield. I see you have found comfort in my home, in my bed sheets, and with my husband." It was Sandra Banks, one of the owners of the luxury residence, the wife of Hamilton Banks, and the mother of his children. She stood tall, dressed in a Eunice Johnson suit. Her hair and makeup were flawless. Her jewelry was a mixture of diamonds and sparkles of gold.

Peyton froze and was unable to speak.

What the hell is she doing here? Hamilton told me she never comes here. What am I going to say to her? What is she going to say to me?

She realized her nude body faced Sandra and she felt like a sixteen-year-old caught sneaking in the house of her boyfriend, as she covered herself with Sandra's expensive sheets.

Shit, I'm caught. There is no other way around this. I can't explain out of this one. I'm just caught.

Sandra stood in the doorway, eyed Peyton with what she interpreted as vile and disgust, and finally spoke again.

"Oh no, Ms. Stanfield, don't cover up for me. It's insulting."

Peyton remained speechless and Sandra continued.

"You have been having a *grand time* fucking my husband and flaunting with him all over town like he's *your* man for some time now and I'm really not sure what to think of you or what to do with you. I must say your boldness is almost admirable." Her stare was cold, serious, and intimidating.

"Let's see, what do they call women like you, the ones who like to sleep with other women's men because they can't find their own? Oh, I know… they call you *whores* and I don't know about you, but where I come from, *whores* get their asses kicked."

At that moment, Peyton realized the phone rang and it was Edgar, again, attempting to reach her. She knew of the reason for his call. Grateful for the excuse to leave the moment, she reached over, grabbed the phone, and continued to watch Mrs. Banks watching her. In a shaky, raspy voice, she answered.

"Hello?"

"Good morning, Ms. Peyton, this is Edgar from downstairs. I was trying to reach you to inform you Mrs. Banks was on her way up. I spoke with Mr. Banks this morning as he was leaving out and he told me you were still upstairs. When Mrs. Banks came in the building, I thought it best for me to alert you. I'm sorry." Edgar sounded *really* nervous. Peyton wasn't sure if he was nervous about what Hamilton's response would be to him or if he was nervous about what was about to happen between her and Sandra. She quickly determined it was probably a combination of both. She did her best to let him off the hook.

"Its okay, Mr. Edgar. Yes, Mrs. Banks is here and I thank you for your call. Good-bye." She hung up the phone, grabbed more of the sheet for cover, continued to sit upright in the bed, and tried to ready herself for whatever Sandra planned for her.

Where is Hamilton and what does this bitch want? After looking around the room for something she could use to defend herself, if needed, she decided she better face this encounter as if she were not scared. After all, she *was* sleeping with this woman's husband, no matter how badly Hamilton described the relationship. She looked at Mrs. Banks with the same fierce glare she gave her.

"Hello, Sandra."

About the Author

Hunter William has previously written fictional short stories. Her debut novel project, *The Charm Town Series,* casts a spotlight on the challenges and triumphs of students in an urban school setting and opens the conversation around such issues as class, race, and educational inequalities. A lover of traveling, good food, sports, R&B and country music, she resides in Maryland with her family.

Made in the USA
Middletown, DE
03 September 2016